EVEN A
SHEPHERD

RONNIE JOWERS

ISBN 979-8-88685-360-5 (paperback)
ISBN 979-8-88685-362-9 (hardcover)
ISBN 979-8-88685-361-2 (digital)

Christian Faith Publishing
832 Park Avenue
Meadville, PA 16335
www.christianfaithpublishing.com

Printed in the United States of America

CONTENTS

ACKNOWLEDGMENTS

*E*VEN *A* *SHEPHERD* IS my very first attempt at writing a book. I have been thinking about Aaron for decades during my career at Emory University and Emory Healthcare. When I retired in 2016, I thought I would live life a year or so as a retiree and then start this book. However, a major bout with B cell lymphoma cancer in 2018 and a year of recovery halted those plans. Then in late 2019, I broke my arm to the point Emory's trauma surgeon based at Grady Memorial Hospital was recommended to fix my arm. All was going well until the pandemic started in March 2019 and the stainless steel bar in my arm broke in April 2020. The surgeon had to replace all of the hardware from the first surgery and take bone marrow from my hip to pack in my arm to help it heal since it was not healing from all of the chemo. So around the summer of 2020, I was able to start work on this book and worked on it well into 2022 during the COVID-19 pandemic.

I was going to get a significant amount of material from a tour of the Holy Land led by my pastor, Dr. David Jordan of First Baptist Church of Decatur. Unfortunately, the pandemic delayed that April–May 2020 trip. David has been remarkably helpful as I constantly asked for biblical knowledge and insights throughout this writing. His insights and extensive knowledge of the Bible; biblical history; and the lifestyles, knowledge, and cultures that existed during Jesus's earthly time have been invaluable. Thank you so much, David.

Dr. Sylvia Wrobel, the former director of communications for the Woodruff Health Sciences Center of Emory University, is a dear friend I enjoyed working with immensely during my tenure at Emory. She graciously agreed to read my writing and give me her thoughts on whether to continue or stop. I knew she would be honest with me. She encouraged me to continue as I questioned whether anyone would be interested in learning my vision of the shepherd boy's story. She made my day when she told me to keep on keeping on. Sylvia, who is an extraordinarily talented writer, helped me with the book's readability and questioned inconsistencies that found their way into my writing. I so valued each of her suggestions and corrections. Thank you so much, Sylvia.

Sylvia's help extended to Karon Schindler and Rhonda Mullins with whom I had the great fortune to work while at Emory. These two talented ladies worked with Sylvia in communications and publications for the Woodruff Health Sciences Center. I was blessed to get to know them and work with them in my Health Affairs role. They have provided tremendous advice and insight on wording, punctuation, editing, and getting this book to the press. Karon and Rhonda—you are awesome. Thank you for all you mean to me.

Sylvia and Karon recommended I contact another former colleague, Mr. Ron Sauder. Ron was director of communications for Emory University. He has always been a great friend and an accomplished writer. He is now an editor for a self-publishing company and has provided tremendous advice and insights. Thank you, Ron. You are a great friend.

Before any editing and insights by any of the aforementioned wonderful people, my very first draft was given as a gift to my supporting wife, Kay, who has encouraged me for decades to write this book. She knows how I have struggled with whether I should write it, if anyone would read it, and if would it be any good. I asked myself over and over, "Will it be pleasing in God's sight?" Throughout this process, Kay has been supportive and encouraging. With her support, I have learned that the exercise was invaluable in helping me learn more about Jesus, his life, and his impact on my life. Whether anyone reads it or not has become secondary. It has been worth writing for my spiritual growth and reflection. Kay's encouragement throughout is a reflective and constant example of the wonderful, loving, and supportive wife she has always been.

An essential contribution that Kay made is suggesting the title of *Even a Shepherd*. Initially, I selected the title *Mary's Eyes* since the depth and understanding in Mary's eyes were a constant theme throughout the book. However, Kay is right; the story is about the shepherd boy's life who found that God could use even him, a shepherd boy, to tell his story! I thank the good Lord daily for Kay and all of the love and sacrifice she has given and made to make my life, and the lives of our children—Ryan and Ivey; our daughter-in-law Kelly; and our greatest ever grandchildren—Noah, Hannah-Claire, Carter, Caroline, and Edie so very remarkable. 2020 marked our fiftieth year together, with each being better than the one before. Kay, thank you for all of your encouragement every day in everything I do. *I love you very much*, Ronnie.

PROLOGUE

FOR DECADES, I HAVE wondered about the shepherd boy who was visited by the angels announcing the birth of Jesus Christ. He received the remarkable gift of hearing the announcement of the Christ child and then getting to see him and his holy family. But what became of that young boy? Did that night shape his life at all? Did he forget what happened and just move on with his life and its daily pressures? Or, instead, did that one single night shape his entire life? I have wondered what thoughts occupied his thinking as he grew into a young man. I have envisioned him asking, "When is what I saw that starry night ever to come to fruition? Years, upon years, have passed, and still nothing. What did that night, that baby's birth mean? For his birth to be announced by angels and be the focus of a bright star in the sky, a wonder of wonders would surely occur. He was to be great. I just wonder when."

This story is my imagination of that young boy's life and how it was shaped by that night. I followed the Bible and its stories about Jesus. I filled in the blanks with my vision of how those events impacted his life. I tell his story, hopefully, as if he were one of your new friends welcomed into your home, with you offering him some hot apple cider and him telling you, in his own words, a most remarkable story. I hope his story makes you think. I hope it makes you put yourself in his shoes as he ponders what he witnessed and tries to understand what it all meant for him and everyone else—even you and me. I hope it makes you ask questions as you strive to understand its meaning and where you fit in.

A frequently expressed wonder about Christianity is that it is simple enough for children to understand yet so complex that scholars are constantly challenged to understand Jesus's true and full meaning. Jesus can touch everyone—from the young to the old and the uneducated child to the most learned elder, those from all walks of life. This story is of his touching one small, seemingly insignificant boy who started his life tending sheep. My prayer is that his story touches you. I hope you enjoy it. May God bless.

The Census Begins

A decree went out from Caesar Augustus, that
a census be taken of all the inhabited earth.
—Luke 2:2 (NASB)

EVER HAD SOMETHING HAPPEN to you and years, even decades later, you still could not understand what happened, why it happened, or what it all meant? For me, it happened over thirty years ago; and every day since, I have thought about what happened, why it happened to me, what it meant, and how things would be different. You see, in one single, solitary night, a unique star was shining overhead, an angel appeared announcing great tidings, a heavenly choir joined in singing glory to God, and I met the Holy Family and held a tiny baby who the angels proclaimed to be the Christ and my Savior! That night of wonder, miracles, family, awe, tenderness, love, and puzzlement are as vibrant in my mind today as if it happened yesterday. Every aspect is as clear as a bell and replays over and over in my head. Since then, days, weeks, months, years, and even decades have passed with little to nothing to help me understand what it was all about. However, one thing is certain: since that night, my life has never been the same.

Only in the past few years did my clouds of confusion begin to lift. Over the past three or more decades, there might have been a handful of days that passed when I did not think about what happened. Constant questioning filled my days. Despite these never-ceasing questions, recent events have helped make it all come together. The puzzle is becoming a picture. I now rejoice that I better understand and can share what started on that one special star-filled night and was witnessed by a small boy tending sheep in the fields of Bethlehem—me!

The meaning is still not perfectly clear but clearer. There is still much to learn. This is my most remarkable story, a story so powerful that I made a promise to try and share it whenever and wherever I could—to whoever will listen. Many have said it is the greatest story ever told—not because of me or my role but because of the one I met and the life changes he has had on me and our surrounding world. I cannot imagine a more remarkable story. Knowing I was a small part from the beginning to the earthly end humbles and challenges me. My heart is warmed every day with wonder and awe. Now it is your turn to hear. My guess is that, when I finish, you, too, will have questions and much to learn. So please sit back, enjoy your apple cider, and marvel at the journey with me.

I am now nearing the age of fifty. A lot of time has passed—a lot of it with absolutely nothing happening except my questioning and hoping for answers. But I remember it like it was yesterday. It started on a clear, starry night—like most nights in Judea. I was a young boy, only ten years old. Five of my cousins, uncles, and I were doing what we did every other day—tending sheep in the meadows. The evenings were no different either. Our routine was what we did every other night. The cycle never changed. With the dogs' help, we had herded the animals into their large, hollowed caves. With long wooden poles and sticks, we blocked the narrow stacked-stone entrance we had built years and years ago. These gates worked well to keep the animals inside and the wolves away. Only then could we relax, sit around the fire, chat, eat, rest, and sleep as others took turns watching the flock throughout the night. Just because the sheep were in the cave did not mean we no longer had to fight off wolves and robbers. No matter what we did, predators lurked.

Staying alert throughout the night was critical. Sometimes, the urgency would come from inside the pen. Sheep might fall and get hurt—especially a newborn. They are pretty clumsy when young. Males seeking dominance for mating would often lead to fights and wounds. Other nights required us to deliver a newborn. For some reason that I can never understand, it seemed that most births occurred in the middle of the night while most of us were trying to get some sleep. If a lamb were to be born, it seemed it would always decide to do so in the middle of the night. I know that is not true; it just sure seemed that way.

The day that changed my life forever started the same as the hundreds and hundreds before. Neither was the night any different. Thousands of stars filled the clear dark sky. Only a few bleats from the sheep, the crackling of the fire, a few crickets, and our chatter broke the deep silence. Many nights, we hear the howl of wolves, but none made a sound that night. The air was crisp with a slight breeze. Little did we know what was in store for us.

The terrain around Bethlehem is rolling hills filled with rocks. A large number of stones and poor soil make it hard for farmers to grow crops. Winter rains and aquifers provide most of the water for drinking and irrigation. Olive trees are plentiful, as are figs and dates. These trees provide much-needed shade in the hot, dry summer. As we settle around the fire at day's end, we see pastures and meadows with a handful of orchards dotting the surroundings. In the distance, we see Bethlehem and Herodium; and on clear, cloudless nights, we can see Bethany.

Our life was one of routine—tending sheep by day and sleeping on mats on the hard ground at night. The nights were often much cooler than the days since there was not much moisture in the air. We do not have many clouds overhead except on rainy spring days. With few to no clouds, the night sky seems to go on forever. The stars fill the heavens by the thousands—always shining clear and bright. Spending so many nights staring at the stars grows old. However, now and then, one of my fellow shepherds would find a new constellation that we would watch every night to see if it kept its shape. Most days, we were up early getting the sheep out to graze and look for water. During the day, we would stop to eat, most often by ourselves. We spent the days just watching the flock, making sure they were safe and well.

Being separated from others, solitude filled our day. Our companions consisted of dogs and our share of the flock. We had hours on end just to think about life, wondering why God created the world and trying to determine what he expects of us. A constant question was, "God, why are we under such oppression from the Romans and their puppet appointees who rule our homeland?"

As a young boy, I often wondered if King David, who started as a shepherd like me, had herded sheep in these very fields—these same meadows I walked through every day. He, too, was from Bethlehem. I also found myself yearning to be with my friends and playing as if we were the great King David. David gave us plenty of adventures to imagine. We played that we were like him—a young boy, learning to throw a sling so hard and with such accuracy that we could slay the mighty giant Goliath and free our land from its oppressors. Sometimes, we would find ourselves pretending to be young warriors challenging the Philistines. Our imaginations often found us being anointed king and ruling the land, just as he had. Long days with little to nothing to do but watch sheep give you lots of time to think. I guess my main constant thought during those long days was, "Will life get any better than this?"

As the youngest of the shepherds, I was often paired with one of my uncles watching our share of the herd. However, I had hope. One day, when I turned of age, my father, Lucius, would teach me his trade and skills. I would then become a stonemason like him and leave behind the tending of sheep. As a stonemason, I could travel and see more of my homeland and get to know people from other trades and cultures. I would not be so isolated. However, while looking forward to that day, I felt sorry for most of my fellow shepherds who would likely spend their whole lives doing what they were doing today and had been doing yesterday, the day before, and the days and years before that. They had little to no hope of breaking their routine. That made me sad.

Now and then, during the day, we would be with another shepherd or two for our meals. Most of these times arose when another needed assistance with a lamb giving birth, dealing with an emergency, or fighting off an animal or robber attack. Sometimes, a lamb or sheep would get sick or injured, and we would care for them as best we could. The oldest among us, Jerome, had seen almost every sickness or injury one could imagine and was always the first we called for emergencies.

While in the fields, we constantly looked for and removed poisonous plants that the sheep always seemed to find. At times, one or more of the flock would stray. Sometimes, we would see them from afar and could round them up quickly. The dogs were magnificent in bringing strays back to the fold. I always loved to watch them work. More often, as we learned from our frequent counts, one or more was missing. When this happened, one or two of us, along with a dog, would go hunting for the strays in hopes of finding and leading them back to the flock. Most times, we were successful, but now and then, the stray or strays would get hurt or attacked and could not be saved. At times, our work was dangerous, especially if we had to fight off wolves, robbers, or poisonous snakes. The robbers were the worst, being the sliest and most skilled, as they raided our flock for food or milk or to add breeding diversity to their own flocks.

Every so often, usually a time or two per cycle of the moon, we got to go home to rest, sleep in our beds, eat our mother's or wife's cooking, bathe, go to the synagogue, and see our friends. But most nights were just like all the others.

We did have one significant change in our routine shortly before that great night. It seemed all at once that the country's calm and beauty were disrupted by the noise and dust of travelers, animals, and carts. The dust from the roadway traffic filled the air and cast a thick haze over the land. Hundreds, upon hundreds, of people were heading either to our village, Jerusalem, Ein Karem, Bethany, or the other villages or towns in the region. We learned they were coming to be counted in the census that Rome's emperor Caesar Augustus had mandated.

A few years prior, Caesar declared that all citizens living in Rome's occupied lands were to be counted in their ancestral homes. After years of preparation and instructions filtering into the outer reaches of the Roman Empire, the time had come for those in our region to be registered. Bethlehem is known as the City of David. Overnight, it seemed all roads leading to this small village filled with those claiming to be King David's descendants. People came from all points on the compass. With King David having had so many wives, his offspring were numerous. Now his distant relatives were heading to my small village of Bethlehem.

My parents were fortunate, however. My father was also a descendant of King David, so he did not have to travel long distances to be counted. My parents would lose some work time waiting for their turn to register. But in the end, they could still sleep in their own beds and do most of their jobs while others just waited and waited. I wondered if my folks would meet any relatives they had not seen in a long time. Maybe they would meet some new kinfolk. Seeing the crowds passing by assured me that little Bethlehem would be filled with huge numbers of King David's family.

The travelers arrived in every way imaginable. Most walked. Many carried children. Some were fortunate to ride donkeys. The most fortunate were able to ride in a cart pulled by their mule, burro, or ox, carrying them and their families. All brought their possessions. They were coming to stay for a while. No one knew how long the census would take.

The government required that a census be taken every fourteen years. For most, this was the first census any of the citizens could remember. While not sure of the process, all were certain of one thing—the outcome would not be for their benefit. The citizens, though free, felt that their lives were not much different from those of the oppressed region's slaves.

Rome had appointed Herod the Great as "King of the Jews." As king, Herod ruled with absolute power and control. Though Herod was a Jewish-born citizen appointed by Augustus to rule the Judean and Palestinian lands, he became a tyrannical dictator. His key focus was to please

Rome and elevate his power, prestige, and control. He ruled by assessing excessive taxation on his citizens. His constant exertion and enforcement of his oppressive power kept the Jewish population of Bethlehem and the surrounding Judean homelands obedient and subservient. His word was law, whether it be a command or a whim. His ever-present army kept everyone firmly under the controlling thumb of governmental rule.

The travelers were confident that the underlying reason for the census was to extract more taxes from them to further swell Herod's and Rome's coffers. With the information and addresses gathered during the census, Caesar and Herod would now know how many people lived in the land and where. The citizens would now be easier to find, making the collection of taxes more efficient and effective. Everyone grumbled about having to make the long, dusty journey knowing that they would be poorer on their return and throughout the coming years. Life was already burdensome and oppressive enough—the census would only make it worse.

Another reason for everyone's discontent was that no one knew how long they would be required to stay in their ancestor's land. How long would they be away from their occupations and their ability to make a living? The census could take days, weeks, or possibly months—no one knew. Much depended on the individual census takers and how hard they wanted to work or how difficult they decided to make the process. The census takers were in charge and would move as fast or as slow as they chose in recording the citizens. One thing was clear. Having not done the census in fourteen years meant almost everyone, including the census takers, was doing this for their first time. Prior experiences or procedures were not in place to make the process any easier. Most commoners worried that speeding up the process would require paying the census taker a bribe—an expenditure most could not afford. The dread of waiting in long lines and staying for extended periods from their homes and jobs was evident on everyone's faces and in their gait as we watched the caravans pass by. It was not a joyous time.

For us shepherds, a new danger surfaced. We now had to ensure that the travelers did not steal a lamb or goat for food. Further, the theft of an animal could help them meet their sacrificial obligations. The Jewish people were required to make sacrifices to God by giving a portion of their possessions—typically, animals, crops, or money. Stealing from our flocks meant they did not have to buy a sacrificial animal from the synagogue or temple merchants. Once on the temple grounds, the prices become exorbitant. Stealing from us was far cheaper. Most of the road's traffic was during the cooler morning hours, though some headed to Bethlehem throughout the day. As the day wore on, the fields and our herdsmen's lives slowly returned to normal, but our attention remained heightened to the new passing traffic.

A Shepherd's Life

In that region, there were shepherds living in the fields, keeping watch over their flock by night.
—Luke 2:8 (NRSV)

AS THE DAY TURNED to evening and then night, all was calm—no winds, no howling wolves—just a clear, rather cool night. The sheep were in the caves, and the entrances were secure. Before housing them for the night, some of my brethren and I had swept and shoveled out dung from the previous night. This daily chore that we all had to share was, by far, our least favorite. The dogs gathered around the fire with us. As usual, we spent our fireside time talking, singing, stargazing, or just daydreaming. Some of us fell asleep while others kept watch. A few hours later, we would swap roles.

Several hours after sunset, the only thing we noticed different from any other night was a star shining brighter than usual. It seemed that, by the hour, the star got brighter and brighter. Before long, it lit the whole countryside. Though the far horizons were now more visible, the star's beam seemed to focus on Bethlehem. Our cave and camp were in a valley lower than Bethlehem. The star brightened the entire village above us.

Bethlehem was our home when we got to go there. My home was on the north side of town between Bethlehem's center and Jerusalem. Jerusalem, the nation's capital, was about a half day's journey north. Our flocks were south of the village, only an hour or so away. My mother, Deborah, and my father, Lucius, kept our house. Requests for father's stonemason services were abundant in Bethlehem and the surrounding villages. However, most of his work focused on Jerusalem or Herodium, as the government routinely conscripted him to work on governmental projects.

At times, his work required him to be away from home for days at a time. However, we were fortunate that most of his work was on the aqueduct, which started in the spring outside Bethlehem and carried water to Jerusalem. Though he did labor throughout Jerusalem, most of his government-required work was on King Herod's Herodium with its fortress and mansion. Herodium was palatial. The entirety of this residence, Herod's retreat, was man-made. Herod had built a mountain taller than the Great Pyramids in Egypt and then cast his splendid buildings across its top. We have never seen the Great Pyramids, but knowing Herod's colossal ego, no one doubted the claims. Herodium was so tall that it was easy to see on the southern horizon of Bethlehem. Most in our little village commented that Herod was surely looking down on us from his lofty heights with all his power, wealth, and contempt. We were nothing more to him than his poor, inferior subjects.

Despite Herod's condescension, we were fortunate that Jerusalem and Herodium were close enough that Father could spend most nights at home with his family. Bethlehem was a small village that only a few hundred citizens called home. I had not been there since the census caravan started, but I could imagine that Bethlehem had never seen crowds like it was experiencing with all those travelers.

As the star grew brighter and brighter, we wondered what was its cause. Townspeople often talked about meteors or comets streaking across the sky. Over the years, we have seen thousands of these shooting stars in our immense open sky. This star, however, was unlike any we had ever seen. It was not moving but just getting bigger and brighter from its single, almost straight-up point in the sky. As the night drew on, it continued to grow in brightness. We questioned if the star was actually two or more stars drawing closer together than usual. If so, how many stars could possibly be coming together to create such brightness? Was it two, ten, one hundred? Maybe even more? Regardless, we had never seen anything like it.

Jerome noted that the star sure made it easier to protect the flock and spot predators. The land was much like it appears at dusk when we could see far more than at night. Talking around the fire was more interesting as we sat in the eerie glow. This night, however, found most of us just gazing into the sky and its bright star. After growing bored looking up, we went back to our routines of checking on the sheep and wrapping up the day's duties. Surely, the sky would return to normal soon.

Two of us were happy. This would be their last night on shift, and the two on leave would be returning to relieve them early the next morning. Shepherds' work was long and tedious, basically an around-the-clock duty. Each morning, we found ourselves already looking forward to nighttime when we could talk with the others, enjoy the cool, and just relax. Each of us found ourselves thinking, "Just one more day, two more days, whatever—until my chance to go home arrives." It was a lonely, tedious, and thankless job.

However, among the shepherds throughout the region, we were the lucky ones. Our flock was notable because our lambs were to be those sacrificed in the temple, especially during Passover and the other major festivals. Our flock's grazing land was more fertile and nearer a slow-moving stream than most other flocks. The other herders constantly had to move their flocks to greener pastures and search for still waters. At night, most herdsmen slept in the fields with their animals. Most nights for us, we kept our flock in the caves protected by the stoned entrances. The temple and synagogue officials who employed us had arranged these benefits. Our flock was handpicked to breed the most perfect, the most unblemished sheep and lambs. Our flocks must be worthy of their owner's sacrifice to God. The sacrificing of our animals cleansed and washed away the sins of their donating owner and family.

When a new lamb was born, we would wrap that lamb in swaddling clothes to protect it from injury and blemish until it was stable on its feet. Newborn lambs are clumsy and frequently fall. The clothes helped keep them from cuts and bruises if they tumbled against the cave's rough rock walls or on the many rocks in the fields.

Our pay was possibly slightly better than that of the other shepherds. We were not sure. This common assumption led to envy among the other herdsmen. However, those same herdsmen would strive mightily if one of these special flocks had an opening for another shepherd. These jobs seldom came open, and when they did, they were usually and quickly filled by family members of the herdsman who had turned ill, had an accident, or had died. The Temple flock, our name for them, had been shepherded by my relatives for decades.

The Torah spoke of several shepherds as heroes—Abraham, Isaac, and David, to name a few. Despite this history, shepherds were considered among the lowest of the low by the townspeople. In the social order, we were very near the bottom. As a workforce, we generally received no education. We made our living doing the most basic and menial manual labor—watching, herding, shearing sheep, and scooping their dung. Our job was to take care of sheep—the dumbest of animals. We were always dirty and smelled like the animals we kept, which was always foul. Being in the fields for days on end, we lacked exposure to the daily and weekly events of the town and the country. So we had little knowledge or experience to have meaningful conversations with those from other trades or the townspeople. Our fellow citizens from Bethlehem did not want to ask about the monotonous routine of being a shepherd. The region's merchants and skilled tradesmen—the millers, bakers, weavers, carpenters, stonemasons, and potters—were considered a class superior to ours. The fishermen, farmers, and shepherds helped make up the lower tier. However, the shepherds were the lowest of that low because of skill level, unkempt appearance, and lack of visibility in the community. The constant smell of fish and sheep further isolated the fishermen and shepherds from the townspeople.

In addition, many herders were thieves and could not be trusted. As I mentioned, we were fortunate to keep our flock in one general area throughout the year. The less fortunate herdsmen constantly looked for new pastures and water for their flocks. This hunt required them to move their flocks over great distances to keep them nourished. Often, this meant encroaching on the property of others which then led to fights and hatred. Thank goodness we did not have to exist like that. Though we had to move our flocks throughout the countryside during the day, most nights, we were able to bring them back to the cave where we were tonight. We could always breathe a little easier when we could herd them here. The chance of predators, losing a sheep, or having harm come to some of them was much less here. Despite this difference, we were still shepherds and grouped with the lowest of the low—the downcast of society. Even the widows and orphans were considered more worthy. People tended to care for those who had lost loved ones. Instead, we tended to ourselves and our sheep.

CHRIST IS BORN

Do not be afraid; for behold, I bring you good news
of a great joy which shall be for all the people.
—Luke 2:10 (NASB)

As THE STAR BECAME brighter and brighter, our conversation grew with excitement and wonder. All of us were looking up when it happened. In the blinking of an eye, the entire sky became so bright that we had to squint and shield our eyes. Some immediately cowered, with hands over their heads, and crouched as low to the ground as they possibly could. One fell prostrate on the ground yelling for help as if anyone could do anything. I stood there speechless, staring into the brightness.

As our eyes adjusted, we could see an angel floating above us, surrounded by pure white light and clothed in a long white flowing gown of lace. He held one hand over his head and the other across his waist. Then looking down as if at each of us individually, he said in a strong and clear voice, "Do not be afraid. I bring you good news of great joy which shall be for all the people, for today in the City of David, there has been born for you a Savior, who is Christ the Lord. And this will be a sign for you: you will find a babe wrapped in swaddling clothes lying in a manger."

Then, immediately after the angel finished, a chorus of seemingly hundreds of angels joined him singing, as if in one voice, "Glory to God in the *highest* and on earth peace, goodwill toward men." The choir seemed to wrap around us from our far left to our far right. Their clothes were blazing white—so radiant. Their voices were as one—pure, clear, full of harmony, perfect. Then as suddenly as it had started, it was over. In the blink of an eye, the angel and choir were gone. All that remained was the one star's brilliance and an eerie silence. Otherwise, the night was like the angels had never appeared. If anything had changed, the star seemed to be even more focused on Bethlehem than it had been just moments before.

For a short while, we just sat or stood there looking up into the sky, wondering what had just happened and what it all meant. The angel's ringing pronouncement, the tremble caused by the harmony, and the depth of the choir's singing had vanished. Quietness enveloped us as we sat there, mouths agape, staring into the heavens. Finally, Jerome spoke while turning to look at us. He questioned, "Did each of you see and hear what I just saw and heard?" We all turned to Jerome and nodded—too dumbfounded to speak. Finally, Jerome, our lead head shepherd, said, "We should go find the babe."

Benjamin, my teenage cousin, blurted, "But who will watch the sheep? I do not want to stay behind. I want to see this baby, the one the angel told us about. I want to see my Savior!" Immediately, all joined in saying that they did not want to stay behind either. Each of us was so excited to see this wonder. "But who will watch the sheep?" asked Benjamin again.

After a few moments of thought, Jerome said we had a few options. We could draw straws, and whoever gets the shortest straw could stay here with the sheep. No one liked that idea, afraid they would pull the short straw. Jerome then optioned that we could take the sheep with us. We had 182 sheep and lambs. Many of the ewes would give birth over the coming months leading into the spring. In Bethlehem, there are always sheep and other animals roaming the streets. Plus, we were going to a stable that most assuredly housed other animals. The citizens are accustomed to having animals everywhere. Jerome added we would fit right in.

Nathan, my uncle, jumped in saying, "But we have a handful of newborn lambs. The lambs alone, not counting the flock itself, will greatly slow us down in getting there. We are surely not the only ones who see the star shining above us or have heard the angels. Their announcement was that this child was for all people. A large crowd will be gathering to see the baby and his family. It will be hard enough for us, as smelly shepherds, to get close enough to see anything! Having a flock of sheep and lambs with us will make it almost impossible."

Jerome, scratching his beard, turned to look to the heavens and then to the flock. He mumbled that the sheep were still asleep and calm, saying, "Look at them. They are totally unfazed by what happened. Neither the angel's appearance, the bright light, nor the chorus' singing that was so penetrating to us has spooked them. Is that not amazing? It is as if nothing happened." Turning to us, Jerome added that the sheep were in their walled stone enclosure with the strong limbs blocking the entrance. None of us had heard any wolves that night.

He then excitedly shouted his decision, "Something special and wonderful just happened. We, all of us, must see what the angel proclaimed. Who are we to ignore God's messenger? This baby must be the Savior for whom we have been waiting. Tonight, our people's centuries of hope and waiting have been answered! All of us must go! If something happens to the sheep, the others who saw the angel and heard the chorus will surely tell the religious leaders of the wonder we have witnessed. However, most assuredly, the religious leaders were the first to hear the message. There had to have been many—who knows—maybe hundreds.—who saw and heard what we witnessed. If so, all will understand why we had to leave. All will agree they would have done the same. Surely, the religious leaders will tell us not to worry. They will agree that we had to rush to see our Christ child. We will be forgiven if something happens."

"Nathan, I agree we do not want to be slowed moving the flock to the village and then having to struggle to get close to the manger. We must hurry! We will leave them here! If we hurry, maybe, just maybe, we can be there before too many of the other townspeople arrive." With that, the six of us quickly checked the cave's stonewalls and its barricades confirming all the animals were safe. With that, we hurried off to Bethlehem.

My name is Aaron. I was the smallest and youngest of the six. I had turned ten only a few full moons ago. Our small band of shepherds consisted of males of all ages. Some wanted to run. Others needed to walk with the aid of their staff. We stayed together, walking as fast as we could. As we neared Bethlehem, I said in my loudest but hushed voice, "How will we find the babe? There are so many places to look."

Malachi, another uncle, said, "We must just trust and believe. The angel told us to go to the City of David. Even now, the star seems to be more focused on one part of Bethlehem. Maybe we go to where the star shines the brightest. The star's appearance on the same night as the announcement must be all part of God's plan. I believe the star will show us the way. Plus, we can follow the others who heard the angel's announcement. There will probably be a large crowd of those closer to the manger than we were, especially with all those in the village for the census. They will already be gathering. They have had quite a head start on us. We will just look and listen for that crowd and their excitement. My biggest worry is whether the crowd will let a bunch of shepherds get through to have a glimpse of the baby.

I cannot wait to see this child. Can you believe it? The Savior, our Christ, the One for whom we have been waiting so long, has been born in our small town of Bethlehem, the village closest to our fields and flocks. Unbelievable! And to think, the angels and the choir included us in their announcement. They appeared to us, a small group of shepherds. Who would have thought it? We are truly blessed.

Let us try and walk faster so we can join the others. Before this night is out, we will see our Savior!"

As we entered Bethlehem, I was, at first, shocked by the stillness all around. There were no crowds, no excitement. Everyone seemed to be asleep. Where were the others searching for the baby? Why were they not exploring every part of the town as we were? The Savior of the world had been born in their small village. Surely, the angels had told others about this wonder—this miracle. After a while of looking and growing frustrated, Jerome held up a hand, told us to stop, and offered up a prayer to the angel, "Heavenly host, you told us of great tidings and the birth of our Lord and Savior. Please show us the way."

As he finished, but without the ability to follow a crowd, we decided to let the starlight guide us.

As we wandered the streets trying to follow the star's beam, we often lost it behind buildings and bends in the roads. Finally, we came to a small home with an attached stable and cave. It was like most of the other homes in the village. It was not all that different from my own home further northwest. As we looked over the stable's fence, we saw a young girl sitting on a bed of hay holding a baby. Beside her was an older man looking lovingly at his new family. Beside them were some sheep, goats, a cow, and a donkey. A nearby water bin and a stone manger served as the animal's food and water source. A single torch and the gleam of the overhead star made the couple and their baby visible. After rocking the babe in her arms, the young mother leaned forward and placed him asleep in the animals' food trough. Peering into the manger, the father wrapped his arm around the mother and gave her a gentle hug. Both smiled.

The couple seemed unaware of us standing outside the gate—oblivious to our gaze and the looks on our faces which must have been full of wonder, puzzlement, joy, and hope. After a moment, the man, leaning on his shaft, looked about and saw us staring expectantly. Seeing us, he smiled, bowed slightly, and motioned for us to come close. As we opened the gate, the young mother heard us, looked up, and smiled. We slowly and ever so quietly entered, making our way to see The Holy Family.

After only a moment that seemed like forever, Jerome said, "An angel and then a chorus of angels came to us in the nearby fields and told us about the birth of a babe that we would find here in Bethlehem. The angel said that we would find the babe wrapped in swaddling clothes, lying in a manger—just like your baby. Is this him? May we see?" The mother looked up lovingly at each of us and said, "Yes, please come. Come see Jesus."

She slowly removed the wrappings from around the babe's head and showed him to us. He looked like every baby I had ever seen. Small, wrinkled, eyes closed—oh so tiny. As we watched, I was struck by how quiet, peaceful, and magical the moment and scene were. All we could do was stand there, looking into the parents' faces and the face of that newborn baby. It was so hard to believe that we were looking at the child who would grow to be our Lord, our Christ, our Savior.

The mother and father surely noticed a tear or two on the cheeks of these roughened and hardened men who lived among the animals. They undoubtedly saw our awe. I felt sure they understood that we were witnessing the answers to our people's prayers over many centuries. Our Christ had been born and was lying in these humble set-tings—right there in front of us. The world would now change. This little baby would fulfill all of our hopes. To this day, I am still moved and awestruck by the wonder and magnitude of that moment. Hardly a day afterward have I not relived that wonder. And to think that God chose me to witness his Son's arrival.

After a long moment of quietly taking in the moment, I blurted out, "My name is Aaron. You told us his name—Jesus. What are your names? Why are you not in a warm house and bed? Why are you out here with the cow, goats, and sheep?"

Jerome jumped in, shooshing me to be quiet, saying I was asking too many questions. But the young mother looked at me tenderly, with the most loving and under-standing eyes I had ever seen, saying, "Yes, his name is Jesus. My name is Miriam, but please call me Mary. Most people do. This is my husband, Joseph. We have traveled the past nine days from Nazareth to be part of the census. My con-dition slowed us down. We did not get here today until it was already past sundown. This house belongs to Joseph's uncle. When we got here, other relatives here for the census had already filled the house. We tried to find other places to stay. However, the many citizens who came to be counted have filled the inns. There were no rooms available for us. Joseph's uncle offered to move some of the relatives out of the house since I was with child, but we refused. This stable was offered, and we said yes. Shortly afterward, it came time for Jesus to be born. Some of Joseph's aunts and nieces in the house helped as midwives. Jesus is my firstborn. The ladies who helped went back to their beds shortly before you arrived. See, it all worked out just fine, and you were able to be here and celebrate with us."

As she spoke, Jesus cried and tossed. I could not help it. "Can I hold him?" I blurted out excitedly.

Jerome snapped, "Aaron, no!"

But Mary whispered softly, "Of course, Aaron, you can hold him. Jesus, this is Aaron." Handing him to me, she said, "Be gentle."

I answered, "I will. I will. I hold my baby brother and sister all the time. I know what to do. I will be careful."

He was so tiny. His sounds were like cooing doves. His cries were so soft—softer than the baby lambs we kept, softer than the donkey, goats, and the cow that surrounded him in the stable. As I rocked him back and forth, I was pretty sure he smiled at me. I looked at his mother and father beaming. As I held him, I could only think that I was holding the hope that my ancestors and all the people of my day had been anxiously expecting. From the ancient days of Abraham, we have been waiting and wishing. Now our wait was over! Am I the first to hold him other than his mother, his father, and the midwives? What a miracle was in my arms.

Mary, who could not have been more than a few years older than me, spoke little and smiled often. Her look took each of us in. The peace in her eyes was so genuine, deep, and touching—even after all she had been through that day. She had traveled to Bethlehem, tried to find a place to stay only to be rejected over and over, settled on a stable, gave birth, cared for her new baby boy, and now greeted strangers. She must have been exhausted and relieved that Jesus was born healthy. But she still welcomed us with tenderness. Thinking back on that night, the one thing that I cannot forget was her compassion. She instinctively seemed to understand our awe, our joy, and our being blessed by the moment. She made all of us feel so welcomed. We were not just strangers who happened to come by. We were as if long-lost friends for whom she cared deeply. I will never forget her. Her peace created in me a memory of contentment and deep joy that I carry to this very day.

In the wonder of the moment, I guess my enthusiasm as a young boy came out once again as I asked, "Jesus—that is such a common name. Why Jesus? The angel said he was to be a Savior, Christ the Lord. Why name him Jesus? That's not a very special name for our Savior."

Again, she giggled, saying, "Just like an angel told you about Jesus being born and that you should come here to see him, a messenger also came to me. He said my son was to be our Savior and that we should call him Jesus."

Joseph added, "Aaron, I, too, had a dream with an angel coming to visit me. He said that this little boy's name was to be Jesus and that he would save people from their sins." A moment later, Joseph added, "You said that an angel and chorus announced that you would find the Christ Lord here, and you came?"

Jerome stood, uncovered his head, and placed both palms over his heart. After bowing his head, he said, "Yes, the angel was bathed in a great, bright light and spoke so clearly, as if talking to each of us, saying good news and great joy had come for all people. A Savior had been born here, and we would find him wrapped in swaddling clothes lying in a manger. When the angel finished, an angelic choir filled the sky, singing of the peace and goodwill that has come to the earth. Oh, how I wish you could have heard them. I have never heard such a beautiful sound—such harmony, such clarity, such power—the voices of many sounding as one. Then just as quickly as they had come, they were gone.

"Once our shock wore off, we rushed here to find you and your baby. Truly, you are blessed to be Jesus's parents—God has chosen you to raise and nurture our long-awaited Christ. Over the centuries, our people have been praying for your child to come. And here he is—the one we have been waiting for, *for* so, so long. You will raise him to greatness. Holy of holies! His coming is truly good news for everyone. Thanks be to God. Blessings be on each of you." With that, Joseph and Mary looked at each other, seemingly in awe of what Jerome had said. I wondered if they grasped all that was happening to them, who was now sleeping in my arms, and what lay in store for them and the world. Little did any of us know how much our lives would change from this moment on.

After another long moment of wonderment and silence taking in this remarkable scene—the baby, Mary, Joseph, the star's beam, the sounds, the manger, and the smells of the stable—Jerome said, "We must go now and let you rest. We need to check on our flock. Blessings to you. Thank you for welcoming us so warmly. Aaron, give Jesus back to Mary." As I carefully and slowly handed Jesus back to Mary, I excitedly asked, "Can I come back to see Jesus again tomorrow?" Mary laughed and smiled, saying, "Jesus will be looking forward to seeing you, as will Joseph and I. Come when you can."

On the way back to the flock, we marveled at what we had experienced and who we had just met. The star continued to light the countryside, making our path easier to travel. After walking a while in deep thought and silence, we finally started saying how stunned we were that no one else had come to the stable while we were there. It seemed that no one else had witnessed this most glorious night. Could it possibly be that we were the only ones to whom the angels came with such news? If so, why? Why us and why only us? Why not the religious leaders, the wealthy merchants, or the educated? Even Joseph's relatives were not there, amazed at the child? Did they not know who had been born in their very own stable? Did they think this was just any other newborn? Did it just seem like just another day and night to them—no different from any other? You see, my questioning began that very night and has never ended.

Thank goodness we were right. The sheep were safe and asleep. It would not be the same for us. Sleep was hard to come by. We could not quit talking about the angels; the announcement; the singing; the light; and then finding Mary, Joseph, and their baby. Each of us seemed to remember exactly—word for word—what the angel said and what then the chorus of angels had sung. Their words, their song, and their appearance were all burned into our memories. Slowly, one by one, we fell asleep amazed at what had just happened.

The following day, we woke excitedly talking about the night before. Many new questions had come to mind as we reflected. Mainly, we could not figure out why the angels had come to us. Though we were fortunate to shepherd the lambs that the priests would sacrifice, we were still lowly shepherds. We smelled like animals. We did not bathe often. We had to stay in the common areas of the temple and were behind in learning to read and write or learning a trade. So why were we chosen?

With no one else at the manger, was it possible that the angels told only us of Jesus's coming? Or had others received the message but chose to not go see the family? We could not make any sense of where the others were. We also could not understand why God, who sent an angel to tell Mary to name her Son, Jesus, and who had sent us an angelic choir to announce the birth, would not let them be able to find a better place to give birth. After all, he was to be our Savior. God had delivered him to earth. Surely, something better than a stable should be the birthplace of our Christ. I know others think us not very smart, but nothing made any sense.

However, there was one thing on which we all could agree. We were confident that a Savior had been born last night and that when he would become a young man, a little older than me, maybe around Mary's age, people would begin calling him their Christ and their Lord. He would be known as our Savior, and he would make us the chosen people whom God had promised Abraham. We smiled at the thought that he would send the Romans back to Rome. We jumped for joy and danced jigs that Judea, Galilee, Samaria, and all Roman-occupied lands would once again be independent. In our lifetimes, the Promised Land would once again be ruled by Jewish law, Jewish practices, and Jewish righteousness. The Jewish people would finally have their Savior. We could not wait to see what the next fifteen years or so would bring—what this tiny baby would make happen as he grew into manhood. We knew we had to wait a while, but, hopefully, before we knew it, the wonder of Jesus would be seen by all, and God's Savior would free his chosen people! As the saying goes, our joy was overflowing. Hope was alive!

THE NEXT DAY

You will find a baby wrapped in clothes.
—Luke 2:12 (NASB)

Mary treasured up all these things,
pondering them in her heart.
—Luke 2:19 (NASB)

LATER THAT DAY, AFTER cleaning the stalls of dung and finishing most of my daily chores, I impatiently begged Uncle Jerome to let me go back to Bethlehem to see Jesus. Grinning, he said, with my elders joining in, "Yes, yes, go! Wish them well for us." I think they all wished they could go with me, though they probably welcomed some quiet while I was gone. I do not think I stopped talking all morning. Once Jerome said yes, I ran all the way. When I got to the stable, it was empty of people but still filled with the animals that were there last night. I went to the adjoining house and asked where I could find Mary, Joseph, and Jesus. The older lady of the house told me they were inside and to come in and see them. When I entered, Mary and Jesus were there. Joseph was in town checking on how the census worked. I asked Mary if she remembered me and if I could see Jesus. She smiled at me, saying, "Welcome, Aaron. Please come in and see Jesus. He has been waiting for you. Do you want to hold him again?"

I quickly said, "Yes, yes, yes!" and rushed over, sitting beside them on the rug on the floor. Mary, cradling Jesus's head, handed me her sleeping baby. Having a younger sister and two younger brothers, I was comfortable around babies. We sat there for a long time, staring at such a little baby. After taking in the surroundings, I said, "These are very nice swaddling clothes. You have wrapped Jesus very nicely."

Mary smiled and asked, "Do you want to hear a story?" I nodded as she began, "I have an aunt who is much older than me. She is even older than my mother. Her name is Elizabeth. She and her husband live near Ein Karem, which is only a few hours' walk from here. But unfortunately, she could not have children when women usually are at the age to have boys and girls."

"You remember the angel that told you that Jesus had been born here and remember Joseph saying an angel had come to him and told him to name our baby Jesus? Remember I mentioned that a messenger angel had come to me too? That angel, Gabriel, said that God had chosen me to give birth to a baby boy who was to be named Jesus. The angel told me that Jesus would be great and the Son of the Most High. He said that my Son would have King David's throne. I naturally was afraid and did not understand how all of this was possible. I was not even married to Joseph yet. The angel said not to worry, adding that, with God, nothing was impossible."

"Angel Gabriel then told me that my elderly aunt, Elizabeth, was also pregnant. With that news, but still so confused and afraid, I just nodded, 'Yes, I will serve God.' Then before I could raise my head, blink, or even snap my fingers, he was gone. The next day, I packed my things and rushed to Ein Karem, to the home of Elizabeth and her husband, Zacharias. Aaron, guess what. Elizabeth, though too old to normally have a baby, was about six months pregnant! When I first saw her, she said the baby in her womb leaped for joy. She and Zacharias were so excited. I wish you could have seen them."

"But Zacharias's excitement was strange. Though he moved, jumped around, and waved his arms excitedly, he did not say a word—not one! If you knew Zacharias, you would know that he is never quiet! See, Zacharias was a priest in the temple. Only once a year, he, like the other priests, was permitted to go into the temple's holy of holies—its most sacred place. While he was in that sanctuary on his special appointed day, an angel—it may have been the same Gabriel who visited me—appeared in his midst and announced that he and Elizabeth would have a son. He proclaimed that Zacharias's son would be great in the eyes of the Lord and they were to name their baby John.

"After getting over his great fear, Zacharias told the angel that he seriously questioned what the angel proclaimed since both he and Elizabeth were too old to have children. It was just impossible. The angel reminded Zacharias that God had sent him to deliver this good news. However, because of his doubt, the angel announced that

Zacharias would not speak again until after John was born. At that moment, Zacharias was struck dumb. When he returned home, Elizabeth was puzzled at the change in her husband, most notably his silence. As I said, Zacharias was never quiet, but that day he was. I can tell you this story because Zacharias wrote down what happened to him so that Elizabeth would understand. Elizabeth told me the story that I now tell you.

"Now back to your comment. Elizabeth was to give birth to John before I was to deliver Jesus. She had been collecting swaddling clothes from Zacharias's older and worn priestly robes. The robes made more clothing than John would need. Elizabeth offered these extras to me for wrapping up Jesus. So that is why some of Jesus's swaddling clothes have such nicely stitched edges and this wonderfully colored embroidery.

"You know, Aaron, I have thought a lot about God's angelic announcements to Zacharias, Elizabeth, Joseph, me, and now you and your fellow shepherds. Each of us is a part of God's plan in the birth of John and Jesus. Zacharias wore these same clothes while performing his priestly duties in the synagogue and temple. Getting to wrap Jesus in swaddling clothes made from priestly fabric makes me think that even Jesus's clothes are part of God's great plan."

I said, "Mary, you have wrapped Jesus in swaddling clothes just like the angel told us you would. When we saw you, the manger, Jesus, and his swaddling clothes, we knew we were where God wanted us to be. As we take care of newborn lambs, we, too, wrap them in swaddling clothes to protect them. We do so to keep them pure and available for God's purpose—as sacrifices for their owner's sins.

"We also frequently have orphaned lambs. They are not really orphans. It is just that for some reason we cannot understand, the mother ewe rejects her baby. If we try to get them back together, the mother will often kick the lamb away. It seems that once a ewe decides to have nothing to do with her offspring, she never changes her mind. The little lamb just cries and cries. If left alone, they will die from starvation, loneliness, and a broken spirit. I recently adopted one of our flock's rejects. I call him Whitey since he is pure white. I wrap Whitey in swaddling rags, feed him, hold him close to keep him warm, and let him hear my heartbeat. At night, we sit by the fire. The other shepherds rub his head, pat him, and let him know he is loved. He sleeps by me. When I call him, he knows my voice and runs to me. Whitey is getting stronger. I think before long, I can return him to the flock. He will be like other orphans we have had rejoin the flock. He will be strong, accepted, and always my friend. He will know he is loved. From now on, when I wrap newborn or orphaned lambs, I will think of how you wrapped Jesus. Doing so will make me think of Jesus as God's little, pure lamb—my friend—someone who will always love me, and someone I love."

Mary beamed. Bowing her head, she said, "What a wonderful story. Thanks for sharing. I will always remember it. Getting back to Elizabeth, I stayed with her until John was born. That was about three months ago. When Zacharias came in to see John and Elizabeth for the first time, he jumped with joy but remained silent. Eight days later, when they took the baby for his circumcision, the religious leaders thought that the parents would name him Zacharias after his father, but Elizabeth said no, 'His name shall be called John.' The leaders looked at each other puzzled. They then questioned Elizabeth and Zacharias, asking if they were positive, saying, 'But, there is no one among your relatives called by that name.' With that, Zacharias took a tablet and wrote, 'His name is John.' As Zacharias showed the tablet to the astonished leaders, his mouth was opened, and his tongue loosened.

"And, Aaron, opened it was! Zacharias let out such a scream of joy and celebration that I am surprised that you did not hear it in the fields surrounding Bethlehem. He was so excited. He shouted his thanks and praises to God, saying he would never, ever doubt God and his power again! Never! He must have shouted, 'Never,' a dozen times or more! All Elizabeth, I, and those who came for the ceremony could do was laugh and clap our hands in joy. He was a sight!

"After getting his new family safely and comfortably back home, he rushed back into the village yelling, singing, and grabbing everyone—telling them of his great news. His friends were shocked that he could speak again, asking how it was possible. He told all who would listen to the whole story from the angel's visit and message to his doubting, the angel's reprimand, his being struck dumb, and the day's events in the synagogue. Now, in his old age, he was finally a father and could speak again. He told them the angel foretold that John would be a prophet like Elijah preaching repentance so that the people would turn to righteousness. John was to make people ready to receive and witness the Lord. John's purpose was to prepare the way for the coming of the Lord. I guess Zacharias had nine months of talking bottled up. For now, it seemed like he could not quit talking. As he left each group of listeners, he warned them to never ever doubt God! Now, Aaron, is that not a great story?" I nodded and smiled. I could not quit nodding and smiling—beaming all the while.

As I thought about her story, it made me curious. "Can I ask you something else?"

Mary said, "Aaron, you can ask me anything."

I started, "Mary, I hope I know how best to ask this. Getting to be Jesus's mother is so special. You are the mother of our Savior. His birth was announced to us by angels. The good news of his birth filled the skies. It does not seem that anyone else heard that message, but we heard it, and everything the angel announced has come true. I know you are blessed to be our Savior's mother. Do you know why God picked you?"

Mary just shrugged; pursed her lips; and, after a long while of thinking, said, "Aaron, you cannot imagine how much I have asked myself that very question. Why me? I am just a young, poor girl from a town even smaller than Bethlehem. In all of Galilee, Judea, Samaria—in all the Promised Land—surely, there are more learned, more spiritual, more religious, more worthy girls than me. Honestly, Aaron, I do not know the answer to your question."

I blurted, "Well, to me, you will be the perfect mother for Jesus. Just look at how you love him and how you make people feel so comfortable around you—what a wonderful lesson that will be for Jesus. He will learn so much from you. I guess, with him being our Christ, you will learn a lot from him too! Watching and helping him fulfill what our ancestors have been expecting all these years will be wonderful. You are truly blessed!"

I continued, "You said you were afraid when the messenger told you that you would give birth. Are you fine now that Jesus is here?"

Mary raised her eyebrows and, after a long thoughtful pause, exhaled, saying, "Aaron, you have no idea how afraid I was. The angel's first words to me were, 'Do not be afraid.' That was hard to do. I was so frightened, but as the angel spoke, a calm, comfortable peace filled my heart despite hearing what seemed impossible. Gabriel said that I had found favor with God and that the Lord was with me. I do not know what I did to find favor in God's sight, but that is what he said. I felt—no—I knew that he was sending me a message from God. With that peace and calm, before I knew it, I was saying, 'Yes, here I am, the servant of the Lord.' With those words, the angel left and I was all alone.

"Aaron, after the angel departed, I guess reality set in, and I realized what life could be like for Joseph and me. Here I was going to be pregnant with a baby. We were betrothed but not officially wed. How would Joseph react? Would he even want to still be my husband? What would our parents think? What would they do? And the townspeople! What would they think? Their questioning and spreading the word would be like wildfire. They likely would judge me poorly. There were so many real-life possibilities that could turn out really bad for us—some of them horrible—for either or both of us but especially for me.

"After thinking about all that had happened, I decided not to tell my parents just yet. Instead, I told them that I needed to go with others from Nazareth heading to Jerusalem. This way, I could join them and then walk alone, only another hour or two further, to see Elizabeth. Seeing Elizabeth would confirm that all that had happened was real. I just had to go see her.

"When I got to Elizabeth's and saw she was pregnant, I was convinced that all of the messages were true. I remember being filled with such joy that I started singing a psalm that I had learned as a young child. Some of its words are, 'My soul magnifies the Lord! My spirit rejoices in God, my Savior!' But, Aaron, when I finished singing, I remembered my namesake, Miriam, who first sang this song, and her reason to rejoice. Have you heard the story of Moses and his older sister, Miriam?"

Shaking my head, I responded, "I have heard of Moses, but I do not know about Miriam."

"Well, Aaron," Mary started, "Miriam is one of our true heroines. Our Jewish ancestors had been held captive for four hundred years or more in Egypt. During the latter part of that captivity, the Pharaoh ordered every Hebrew child to be drowned in the Nile River. Miriam's baby brother, Moses, had been born during this time. His family was able to hide him for about three months. However, as Moses grew, it became impossible to hide him any longer. So Moses's mother and Miriam decided to put him in a tar-coated, waterproof bulrush basket. They then cast the basket in the river among the bulrushes near where Pharaoh's daughter, the princess, bathed. Miriam and her mother prayed that the princess would find Moses, pity him, and decide to take care of him. Aaron, what they prayed to happen did! God answered their prayers!

"The slaves attending the Pharaoh's daughter heard Moses crying. After finding him floating in the river among the reeds, they took him to her. The princess recognized him as a Hebrew boy. Miriam, who was nearby listening, rushed to her and asked if she could help find a Hebrew woman to nurse the baby. The Pharaoh's daughter agreed and offered to pay whomever Miriam found to nurse the baby. And guess who Miriam went to get. Moses's mother! Moses's own mother was able to raise her son into manhood!"

"Over time, Moses was instructed by God to lead his people out of bondage and Egypt." I interrupted. "Mary, this is the part of the story I've heard. First, God caused many plagues to torment the Egyptians. Then finally, when the Pharaoh could take no more—he freed our people, letting Moses lead them out of Egypt."

"Yes, Aaron, you are right," Mary said. "Moses led thousands of our people from captivity. However, before they had gone too far, Pharaoh changed his mind and sent his soldiers to recapture them and bring them back. When Moses and his people reached the Red Sea, they thought they were trapped. God, however, was with them. When Moses raised his staff and prayed for God's help, the Lord parted the sea's waters. Our people then crossed to the other side on dry ground with walls of water on both sides. They crossed unharmed.

"When the Egyptians came to the sea, they also tried to cross the sea between the vast walls of water. While in the middle, God released the water, drowning all of them. Our ancestors were now truly free! Realizing their freedom, Miriam took a tambourine or timbrel and led the women in rejoicing by singing and dancing. Part of the psalm she sang said, 'Sing to the Lord, for he is highly exalted!'

"Aaron, Miriam rejoiced in the freeing of our people from bondage. When I finished my song of joy, I realized that my song, too, was one of praise that this baby you hold is to be our Savior and free us from our bondage. God saved our people from Egypt. He now sends a new Savior to free us. I am so happy my parents named me Miriam—Mary.

"Aaron, every day since has not been easy. While pregnant with Jesus, I at times felt poorly, was nauseated, and just had no energy. My condition slowed our journey here. The journey from Nazareth took us nine days when a week is normal. Giving birth was hard. But through it all, my heart is filled with such wonder and joy. Ever since the angel's announcement, I keep thinking, 'This is God's plan.'

God has found favor in me. I have given birth to our Savior—the Savior of all people! It has happened. You are a witness to the start of God's greatest wonder. I am in awe of what God has done already. I can only imagine what he will do through that little boy—and I get to be a part of it! Never could I have imagined being chosen by God. I do not know why he chose me, but I promise you and God that I will do all that I can to be the best mother Jesus could ever have. I am afraid that I may not be worthy. But then I think God picked me! Me—Mary—this young girl sitting here in front of you! I cannot question God. I do not understand his reasoning, but I will do all I can to do my best for Jesus. Aaron, when you pray, will you pray that God helps me be that kind of mother?"

Her sincerity filled my eyes with tears. When I could speak, I said, "Mary, I promise that I will pray every day for you, Joseph, and Jesus. I will thank him daily for choosing you to be Jesus's mother. I will pray that he help you every step of the way. I will also thank God for letting me be a part of this story. I cannot wait to see what happens and what Jesus's future brings as he gets older!"

With that, Mary and I just sat quietly, looking at Jesus. He was asleep. All the while, I could not get over my amazement at how such a young boy, a lowly shepherd, a citizen of such a small village could be a witness to God's newborn son. I saw this baby on his birthday. In all of eternity, I was one of the very first to see our Savior. I was one of the first to hold him, hear him cry, see him open his eyes, yawn, and go back to sleep. I met his parents—Mary and Joseph. I learned about Jesus's cousin John and God's plan for John. I know I grinned from ear to ear when I thought of how happy Elizabeth and Zacharias must be. I remember thinking that I would tell my friends and family about these days—these wonders. I imagined, one day, having my own family and telling my little boys and girls that their father was there at the beginning—that I knew Jesus when he was a baby even younger than them. I could just imagine their surprise and awe. I so looked forward to that day. Through it all, I kept wondering if God had anything else in store for me. Mary and I just sat there for a long while, taking in the moment and its wonders.

As I watched Mary looking at her little boy, I could see why God picked her. She seemed to understand life—why and how things were. Helping God fulfill his plan for her son was her new role. While in great awe of all that was happening to her, she understood and willingly accepted what was to come. She was no more than a girl. So much was being asked of her, but she was willing to give freely. Through it all, she was content. Her presence, peace, gentleness, and serenity amaze me to this day. When she looked at you, she conveyed, "I know you. I care about you. I love you. You are God's child."

Soon after, I told her I must go back to the sheep but would like to come back again if that was okay. She smiled and said, "Aaron, you are always welcome to come and see Jesus any time you can. I know that Jesus is happy to see you too. I know he loves you and likes you being around. Just look at how peaceful he always is when you hold him. Please come again."

THE PRESENTATION OF JESUS

And when the days for their purification according
to the law of Moses were completed, they brought
Him up to Jerusalem to present Him to the Lord.
—Luke 2:22 (NASB)

ND COME AGAIN, I did. One late afternoon when I arrived, Jesus seemed fussy, irritable, and uncomfortable. Joseph told me that today Jesus had turned eight days old. Under the covenant between God and his people dating back to Abraham and per Hebrew law and customs, a Jewish boy was to be presented for circumcision on his eighth day of life. Joseph said that he and Mary had gone to the closest synagogue and found the local rabbi who took Jesus and performed the rite while Joseph helped. When completed, the rabbi gave their son his formal name—Jesus, which means "God saves." Joseph rejoiced, saying, "What a wonderful, glorious day this is! We are so glad, Aaron, you are here to join this happy celebration!"

Every day, I waited for the chance to go and see the Holy Family. Jerome kept telling me that I should not go every day or I would wear out my welcome. So, as hard as it was, I would not go for a day or two. Finally, when I could go, I was so excited. During one of my visits, Joseph was there. He was tall and lanky compared to most Hebrew men. His hands were large and calloused with many cuts and scrapes, undoubtedly caused by his work. His demeanor was mainly quiet and thoughtful. His words were soft to the point I often had to strain to hear him when he spoke. His eyes were dark and deep. His hair and beard were a dark brown with deep waves.

As he fixed a chair for his relatives, he told me he was twenty-five, a carpenter and builder living outside Nazareth. His craft was to make furniture, tools, and framing for doors and roofs. He told me that Mary lived with her family in Nazareth. Usually, a trip from Nazareth to Bethlehem was an eight-to-ten-day journey if you took the safer but longer route. He and Mary had taken the shorter but more dangerous course through Samaria. Mary's pregnancy made a regular weeklong trip take a few days longer. They were fortunate that Mary could make the journey riding a donkey, but she was in a lot of discomfort over the rugged terrain. They often stopped so Mary could stretch her legs and try to get more comfortable. He marveled at how well she did throughout the long journey—never complaining, doing all she could along the way with the food preparations, taking care of the donkey, and doing whatever else she could to help. During their stops, she even helped with the needs of the other traveling families. The roads were filled with travelers heading in every possible direction, most to be registered in the census. Joseph repeatedly voiced his amazement at Mary's strength, positivity, and determination, calling her a remarkable young woman. His pride in her showed in his every word and expression. He beamed whenever he thought about her and his new son.

Since King David was his ancestor, they had come to Bethlehem, the City of David, to participate in the Roman government's ordered census. He was anxious to get back to Nazareth because he had some construction and carpentry projects to finish. A look of worry crossed his face as he explained that he had often worked in nearby Sepphoris, the capital of Galilee, which is a half-morning walk from Nazareth. Sepphoris, a city much larger and busier than Nazareth, had been destroyed earlier that year. Joseph's trade would be in great demand with the reconstruction, but until Herod decided to restore the town, he wondered if any jobs from that area would come his way. It was apparent that Joseph wanted to provide well for Mary and his new son. He spoke of someday having a larger family.

He tried to imagine what family life would be like with one of his children destined to be the people's Savior. Could his family live a typical everyday life? Would Jesus want to learn a trade? Would he be a good carpenter and enjoy construction? His biggest worry seemed to be if he could be the earthly father that Jesus's heavenly Father wanted and expected him to be. As I watched him with his head down thinking and, at times, shaking his head, I could tell Joseph was very anxious about fulfilling his new assignment.

On the one hand, he was anxious about raising not his son but God's Son—the Son of the Creator of the world!

But, on the other hand, he was excited to help usher in a new kingdom through Jesus. Joseph closed his eyes, and I heard him pray, "Dear God, help me be worthy!"

When he finished his prayer, Joseph turned and looked at me. I asked, "The angel told us that Jesus would be a Savior for all people. What do you think that means?" Joseph paused a long time and then shrugged, saying that he too was puzzled by that statement. Nevertheless, he was sure that God had commanded it and that God had great things in store for Jesus. Maybe all Jewish people are what the angel meant by "all people." Maybe, just maybe, the words meant that Jesus was, indeed, here for everyone—no matter their faith, homeland, or heritage. Maybe Jesus was to be Savior for the whole world. He shook his head and laughed, saying, "That is so hard to believe! I guess we will just have to wait and see. Could Jesus really be the Savior for the Romans? Could he possibly be Herod's Savior? Seems so hard to believe! Aaron, I truly do not know! I wish I did. Maybe we will figure it out together as things unfold."

I asked if he thought Jesus would get rid of the Romans so that the Jewish citizens could once again rule as God's chosen people in God's chosen land. After all, Jesus was to be our Savior! Joseph paused and shrugged, saying that he did not know this either, adding, "Aaron, we may just have to take this adventure one day at a time. The angel who visited me said that Jesus was to be Immanuel, which means 'God with us.' The angel who visited you announced Jesus would save people from their sins. Whatever all this means, I know that little baby you have been holding means that the God in heaven is now with us here on earth. Whatever happens, whoever he becomes, whatever role you and I are to play, we are blessed to be a part of what God is making happen. Yes, Aaron, you and I are very blessed, but we'll just have to wait and see what comes."

On the way back to the fields, I could not stop thinking, *God is with us. God is with me. With my family—my fellow shepherds—with all people. Remarkable!* I have gotten to hold him. I have called him Jesus. I have seen him smile. I saw him cry, squirm, be upset, be calm—just like any other baby I had ever seen. He was just like my own baby brother, Simon. Yet he was to be different. This little Jesus was to be great. He was our good news, our Savior, our Immanuel. He is 'God with us.' Those thoughts made my walk back to the flock fly by.

Over the next several weeks, I was able to visit many times. After the appropriate time for Mary to devote herself to her own care and that of Jesus, I noticed that she was more and more active in helping the women of the house prepare meals, take care of the animals, and do the cleaning. She was showing the energy of her youth. I heard her laughing as I neared the house one day. When she saw me, she clapped and motioned me to come, saying, "Aaron, do you want to hear another fascinating story while you rock Jesus? This story is both exciting and disturbing."

I did not want to hear anything that would disturb her, yet I wanted to hear the story she was so excited to tell. So with that, I said, "Yes, please."

Mary started, "Yesterday, Joseph, Jesus, and I went to the temple in Jerusalem for my purification. It has been forty days since Jesus was born. By Jewish law, women who bear a male child are to make offerings for their purification. Joseph and I took two pigeons as our offerings. We, unfortunately, could not afford a lamb, so we offered what we could, the required minimum. After we made our sacrifice and entered the temple's Court of the Women, we presented Jesus to God per the words of Exodus, which tell us, 'Consecrate to me all the firstborn.'

"As we were finishing, an aged man named Simeon came up to us. He said that the Holy Spirit had told him that he would not die until he had seen the Christ. He added that the Holy Spirit had led him to the temple and then to us. He asked if he could hold Jesus. When I handed Jesus to him, Simeon said, 'Now, Lord, you can let your servant depart in peace because my eyes have seen thy salvation, which thou hast prepared in the presence of all people—a light of revelation to the Gentiles and the glory of thy people Israel.' Joseph and I just looked at each other. I am sure our mouths were open. With that, Simeon blessed us and started handing Jesus back to me. As he did, he said, 'Behold, this child is appointed for the fall and rise of many in Israel and for a sign to be opposed. A sword will pierce even your own soul—to the end that thoughts from many hearts may be revealed.'

"Aaron, his words have been burned into my memory. I remember them as if I had said them. He said Jesus was God's salvation. In the same breath, he mentioned all people, Gentiles, and Israel. Gentiles? Can it be that Jesus has come for even the Gentiles? But then he also said that even my soul would be pierced. Aaron, Simeon said these words looking directly at me. He said my soul would be pierced.

He did not mention Joseph. Was he talking directly to me and only me? I do not know what he meant. I was so confused and troubled. After a moment of stunned silence, looking down, trying to take it all in, I looked up to ask him to explain, but he had turned and was lost in the crowd.

"Then immediately as Simeon left, a woman of great age—she must have been in her eighties or more—came to us and said her name was Anna. Anna told us that she has been a widow for most of her life. She said she serves the temple every day and night. She began thanking and praising God, saying that Jesus was the child all were looking for to redeem Jerusalem. Aaron, we were just dumbfounded by both Simeon and Anna. They knew about Jesus. Only God could have told them. We had never seen them before, but they knew! They knew about Jesus and God's plan for him.

"Naturally, Joseph and I did not say much walking back to Bethlehem as we were absorbed in our thoughts of what had happened in the temple. We were just trying to make it make sense. One moment, Jesus was being called the Christ, the Savior, our salvation, and the redeemer of Jerusalem. All things of great joy, wonder, and expectation. In the next moment, Simeon mentions a sword and said that Jesus was to be opposed, that Jesus was to be the cause of the rise and fall of many, and that my soul would be pierced. Oh, what is in store for my son? What is in store for me, and what about Joseph? Oh, Aaron, what will our lives be like as Jesus grows? Can I do this?"

After sitting quietly for a long time, I said, "But, Mary, remember that the angel told us, as shepherds, that they were bringing good news—to all of us! This good news is for all people! That little boy lying right there is Good News! He is the one we have been waiting to come for centuries. All my hopes and those of our people are on seeing what goodness Jesus will bring. Good news! The angels would not have announced it if it were not true. All of their other pronouncements have come true—Elizabeth and John, you and Jesus, Jesus being born, and our finding him in a stable. All are true. They said that great things are about to happen all because of this little boy! I have no doubt. I am positive! Too many angels have told us so. Good news is right here—right there—all in your son, all in Jesus!" On the way back to the fields, I wondered what Simeon meant about Mary's soul being pierced.

THE MAGI VISIT

For we saw His star...and have come to worship him.
—Matthew 2:2 (NASB)

A DAY OR SO after Mary's story about her visit to the temple, I rushed to see them again. This time was very different. As I neared the house, I passed camels and several men who appeared to be servants or commoners. I could not imagine they were from anywhere near Bethlehem or even Judea. They clearly did not look like us. It seemed that wherever they could find an open space outside of the village, the servants were setting up elaborate tents, building fires, and making camp—a camp that looked more royal than anything I had ever seen.

As I got to the front door of the relative's house where the Holy Family was staying, I saw three Arabian men, or what I understood was how Arabian men looked. I had seen travelers from the Far East as they had passed by heading to Jerusalem or Egypt. Many traded spices or salts from the nearby Dead Sea. These men looked like them but were dressed far more royally and acted more regal than anyone I had ever seen. Their clothes were of the finest, elegant, royal silk. Jewels were everywhere, especially on their elaborate crowns. They looked like what I expected of kings and princes.

I edged my way through the servants to the door to see what was happening. I had not heard of Easterners being Jewish, but it was clear they were here to see baby Jesus. I later learned that these men were called magi, which is what I will call them. The three gathered around Jesus and Mary. Joseph stood over to the side. I caught bits and pieces of what they said. I was astounded that they spoke Aramaic, just like us. They announced that they were astronomers—stargazers. In their studies, a strange new star in their west had appeared. Their observances and research convinced them that, after a long journey over deserts and dangerous lands, they would find the King of the Jews.

After traveling for roughly six months, they stopped in Jerusalem, asking where they might find the baby who was born to be 'King of the Jews.' The magi learned from the religious and governmental authorities that the baby was to be born in Bethlehem. They had come here to behold our new King. As they knelt, they asked Mary if they could see him. Mary nodded and turned Jesus so each of the magi could see. They prayed and chanted as they glimpsed the tiny one they had traveled so many months and over such treacherous lands to see. Each extended a hand and touched the baby's hand. Their dedicated focus on Jesus showed great reverence. After a long while, they turned to Mary and then Joseph—blessing each of them. As they got ready to leave, each turned and called for their servants in a language I did not know. Each attendee then retrieved boxes and packages which they laid before their master, their magi. Each man then picked up his package, prayed over it, and presented it to Mary and Joseph as gifts for Jesus.

The first magi said his gift was gold—worthy of a king. The second gave frankincense—worthy of a priest. The third gave myrrh—worthy of anointment. After laying the gifts around Mary and Jesus, they bowed, rose, and then, oh, so quietly, turned and left. Mary and Joseph watched them go with looks of awe, but both nodded as if they somehow understood. I moved aside and watched the men and servants head back to their camp. Each looked at me. One even tousled my hair, but none spoke as they left in quiet reverence.

Standing in the corner as the room emptied, I waved to Mary and Joseph. They waved for me to come closer, but I whispered that they must be tired and excited after the magi and their caravan's visit. I do not know why I whispered—maybe the quiet that lingered in the room just seemed to call for reverence. Anyway, I whispered that I would try and come back tomorrow.

As I walked back to camp, I passed the magi's camp. My first thought was that the Lord had started letting others know the good news about Jesus's coming. The rich, educated, and powerful would now hear about Jesus. The news was beginning to spread—not just known by only a few shepherds and two aged temple worshipers but people from near and far—even from the far Far East. News of the wonder that we witnessed only a month or so ago was finally beginning to spread. Finally and soon, all would hear and know the good news! My second thought was to ask the magi if the star that brought them here was the same star that we saw that night, but I did not. I guess I was afraid to approach men of such wealth and knowledge.

Reentering camp, I told my relatives of the magi, their gifts, and their prayers to Jesus as the new King of the Jews. My fellow herdsmen also wondered if they were Jewish. If not, their presence confirmed that the angels had truly meant all people, regardless of who they were, where they were from, or their religion. That revelation reminded me of what Simeon had said to Mary—that God's salvation, Jesus, was prepared in the presence of all people and would be revealed even to the Gentiles. Knowing that soon everyone would know about Jesus, a new excitement filled our camp. Surely, the rich men from the East would tell everyone they met as they headed home. Maybe they would go back to Jerusalem to tell the officials of their success in finding the new King. Now all officials of every type, whether religious or political, would know. It was going to be exciting to see the joy and celebrations of people from miles and miles around when they learned that their new King had been born in Judea here in my own hometown. Once others heard the news from the educated, rich Easterners, all would believe and start making their way to Bethlehem to see this new gift from God. Soon nothing would ever be the same again.

The Disappearance of the Holy Family

Arise and take the Child and His mother, and flee
to Egypt, and remain there until I tell you; for Herod
is going to search for the Child to destroy Him.
—Matthew 2:13 (NASB)

I worried that Mary, Joseph, and Joseph's family were getting tired of seeing me so often; but you would never know it by the way they welcomed me. However, when I arrived for my next visit, I found they were gone, as were their belongings and their donkey. It was like they had never been there. I asked the owners of the house where they were. They did not know either. They told me that during the night, Joseph had a dream. An angel told him to, in great haste, take the family and leave. Joseph thanked his relatives for their hospitality, hurriedly packed, and left in the early morning hours before dawn. He did not say where they were going. The relatives did not think Joseph even knew where they were heading.

Over the weeks that the Holy Family had stayed with Joseph's family, all had learned of the angels' announcements to Mary and then Joseph. All knew of the heavenly proclamation to us as shepherds. The family knew of our visit to the manger and why I kept coming back. Surely, Mary had told them the stories about Elizabeth, Zacharias, and John. Mary's troubled mind naturally would share their visit to the temple and Simeon's disturbing words followed by Anna's praise. Everyone in town was talking about the majestic royal visit from the Far East's magi. Knowing of these events, Joseph's family wondered if Joseph might just rely on an angel to show them where they were to go. It was possible they were returning home to Nazareth since they had recently been counted in the census. However, deep down, they did not know. The only thing they knew for certain was that Joseph knew they must leave immediately.

I was so sad. I did not get to say goodbye. I did not get to hold Jesus one last time. I did not get to thank Mary and Joseph for their kindness. I know it must have been hard some days to have a young boy come visit so often. Yet they seemed as excited to see me as I was to see them. I did not get to tell them how much I looked forward to holding Jesus and imagining what kind of life he would have. I cried. Actually, I cried a lot. I had made some new dear friends who I would miss terribly.

Going back to daily life as a shepherd without the excitement of rushing to see Jesus was hard. My days continued to fill with new questions. Mostly, I imagined what was to come of Jesus and his family. Was Jesus to be a great orator who drew people to him like water to a sponge? Would he lead great revolts or armies? Would he be a minstrel performing seemingly impossible tricks and stunts that would captivate people into following him? Would he become a Jewish leader well versed in the Torah? Would he lead negotiations with Herod and the Roman government? Would he be a peacemaker or a revolutionary? Where were they?

I did not realize it then, but this separation from Jesus started a whole new phase of my life. I would become consumed pondering innumerable scenarios, trying to understand what had happened and what the future held. What did that night really mean? My idle time watching sheep became filled with these puzzles and my trying to fit the pieces together. Little did I know this would be my new life—asking a new question about Jesus almost every day. My life was one of puzzlement—one big question mark.

I first started wondering when we would begin to hear about John and then Jesus. Yes, both were babies. So maybe in fifteen, surely before twenty, years, we would start hearing great things. We knew the word must be spreading from our constantly telling anyone who would listen. Surely, the magi's words were getting the people excited. There must be others like Simeon and Anna who knew he was out there, and all of them would share what they knew. How many others, like me, knew and were waiting for him? The number would, indeed, soon be in the thousands. All we needed was his call. How many would search throughout the land for him? We had all become a part of Jesus's story. In time, as the word spread, any and everything that Jesus did and said would be known and shared throughout the land.

In no time, we would begin to hear about John laying the path for Jesus's arrival. He would tell all to get ready to follow their new King. The coming fifteen years or so would probably drag by. However, when Jesus was ready, I would be ready. I vowed to stay watchful and prepared— whatever God expected of me, I would do. My daily prayer was that Jesus would use me to usher in his *good news*. I vowed to be ready.

But over the coming weeks and months, our shepherd lives returned to our daily routine—much like nothing had ever happened. Whenever any of the six of us saw someone, we would tell them about what we had seen and heard that starry night and since. However, with Bethlehem being so small, it was not long before everyone had listened to our story. Some believed and shared our story with their friends and neighbors. Many others doubted, saying things like, "Surely, our King would not be born in a stable among animals!"

Some concluded that we had eaten or drunk something terrible that had caused us not to think clearly. Others felt we had dreamed up a good story while sitting around the campfire night after night. They believed after telling it enough that we had actually begun to believe what we dreamed up.

Most wondered if what we said was true, how come no one else in the town or country knew about it? If the angel's and choir's sound was so loud and pure, why had they not heard it? If their radiance was so blinding, how come no one else saw it? How could some shepherds and some mysterious strangers from great distances away see a star that was so bright—one that was so focused right here in their own village—and they had not seen it? Why would only a bunch of herdsmen get to know about God coming to earth? Certainly, their Christ would not be born in Bethlehem of all places. And where were this Jesus and his family now?

Many believed we had experienced something, but most thought it was nothing of real importance. Many other locals questioned why we persisted in telling and retelling a fable. They repeatedly reminded us that today seemed no different than a few weeks or months ago. A common response was, "Go back to work, and forget what you saw or think you saw." Life went on just like it always had. Getting people to believe that their Savior and King was in their midst was going to be more challenging than I ever would have thought possible. Maybe the problem was that the word was coming from us—people who they knew.

When I was first able to go home after Jesus's birth, I was naturally excited to share my story. However, it was not long before most of my family got tired of hearing me talk about that night and my visits. My mother, father, and siblings never witnessed what I did that holy night or get to meet the Holy Family. I could never get them to feel my excitement and wonder as to what was to come. They mostly questioned why I had not come by to see them if I was in the village seeing Jesus.

In hindsight, I should have run clear across town to share with my family. They lived in the village's northwestern corner, the furthest point from the stable where Jesus was born. The shepherd's field was even further south. It was somewhat of an extra hike, but that is just an excuse.

I should have gone to see them. Instead, I guess I got so wrapped up in the moments that all I seemed to care about was seeing Jesus and then getting back to the field and sharing with my fellow herdsmen.

As shepherds, we could relate. We had started, as one, on this most spectacular journey. My excitement was their excitement, and theirs was mine. Nothing else seemed to matter other than getting back with them to share the joy and the new wonders that came with each visit. I am sorry that I did not go to see my family. I should have taken them to meet Jesus. I messed up.

Of my family, only my older brother, Dismas, seemed to be fascinated by what we had heard and seen. He asked me, over and over, to retell my story. Dismas was six years older than me. He worked as a stonemason with my father and was home or gone, matching my father's schedule. When I was not in the field, I lived with my parents and four siblings—Dismas, Helen, Timothy, and Simon. Timothy was five; Helen, three; and Simon, the youngest, just over a year old. We had another sister who would have been eight but was stillborn. Mother still cried at times for Savannah.

Having Simon in the house seemed to make all of us forget any rough or sad days. Simon was the happiest child I had ever seen. He was fun-loving, always with a smile on his face. He had just learned to walk. Maybe run was closer to describing how quickly he could get around and into everything. He and Dismas were incredibly close. Simon always lit up when Dismas came home, as did Dismas when he saw Simon come ambling to him with his arms open wide, ready to be picked up and thrown into the air before coming down into Dismas's big arms and a huge hug. Our family was loving and close. I so looked forward to the time or two per cycle of the moon that I got to leave the flock, come home, and be with my family.

I also looked forward to the passage of a few years when I would move into manhood. Then my father would teach me the skills of a stonemason, and I would be strong enough to lift and carry the heavy stones and materials. I anxiously awaited for Father to teach me to read, write, and do the math needed for our business. The whole family worked hard.

Many days, we dealt with the constant struggles caused by Herod's Roman-sanctioned tax collectors. They seemed to have an insatiable demand for more and more sacrifices from their citizens, usually in the form of taxes, fines, and fees. Most days, providing tomorrow's meal, lamp oil, or the next candle was a struggle. Yet despite these daily demands, we were happy. Life in our household was good. We felt fortunate that many days we were all together at supper and bedtime. But all was about to change suddenly and horribly.

THE KILLING OF THE INNOCENTS

Then when Herod saw that he had been tricked by the
magi, he became very enraged, and sent and slew all
the male children who were in Bethlehem and in all
its environs, from two years old and under, according
to the time which he had ascertained from the magi.
—Matthew 2:16 (NASB)

A FEW MONTHS AFTER Jesus's birth and a few weeks
after the magi's visit, I was in the fields tending the
sheep. A small regiment of soldiers passed by our
flocks on the road heading east-west into Bethlehem. They
looked serious; but, as I had come to learn, all soldiers,
whether Herod's or those from Rome, always looked serious. To our horror, we later discovered that they entered the
village, dismounted, spread out, and commenced shouting
and waving their swords. Everyone sought shelter. Before
anyone knew what was happening and with no explanation, the soldiers started going house to house, smashing
open doors, and searching for every small boy.

We learned later that they were looking for every boy
aged two and younger. When they found a male child,

they pulled him from the clutches of whoever was holding him and carried him into the street. Then with no signs of mercy, no compassion, or no sense of humanity, they began running their swords through those babies. There were no explanations—just violence and brutality as they killed these small, defenseless young boys in the streets in full view of their families and townspeople. They would kill one and move on, looking for the next child.

Word reached us in the fields that the soldiers had taken Simon and my uncle's youngest son. My uncle and I hurriedly left the sheep in the care of the others and rushed home. As we reached the village, we each went to our own homes. The wailing and crying were unlike anything I had ever heard. I hope never to hear sounds like that again. The soldiers were gone. However, the blood in the streets, the wounds and bruises on the family members who tried to protect their young, and the sight of dead boys still lying in the streets were unbearable. In addition, the streets, businesses, and homes were all in disarray as the soldiers had turned over furniture, broken earthenware, thrown clothes, overturned baskets—whatever they needed to do to be sure that they found every baby boy. Anguish abounded.

My father and Dismas had been working on the aqueduct between Bethlehem and Jerusalem. They arrived shortly before I got there. I witnessed firsthand this terror when I got home to see my mother holding the lifeless Simon. My mother, Deborah, had been home with Timothy, Helen, and Simon when the soldiers came. She alone witnessed the horror of them pulling Simon from her arms, hitting her with the backs of their hands, and violently pushing her away. She watched as they carried Simon crying into the alley and then repeatedly slashed him with their swords. She witnessed them then tossing Simon's lifeless body to the side.

In just a moment, Bethlehem had lost all of its young boys. The horror of the loss, magnified by the memories of Herod's soldier's cruelty and uncaring nature, amplified the constant screams and crying. The incessant questioning of "Why?" flamed the anger that engulfed our once quiet and peaceful village. Happiness was no more.

Over the next few days, the streets remained full of cries and wailings as the townspeople buried their sons, grandsons, cousins, brothers, nephews, and friends. The cleaning of the city streets, walls, and clothing took days. Grief covered the town like a dark, dense, heavy fog. Eighteen young boys had mercilessly been murdered. The anger, cries, and screams continued to flood the air. All were asking why Bethlehem and why only Bethlehem? Why only the smallest and youngest of boys? None of it made any sense.

When soldiers returned days later to the village, the townspeople screamed, "Why?" The soldiers' only reply was, "Those were our orders from Herod. We do not know why. We only know that we would have met the same fate as those babies if we did not obey. We did as we were told."

For most of us, things slowly got somewhat back to normal. Life had to go on. I returned to tending the sheep with my uncles and cousins. My relatives had covered my shifts while we mourned and buried Simon. Some in the town recovered better than others. For most, daily life and activities returned though without the joy that had once filled the town. Healing would be a long time coming.

Some, however, turned bitter and harbored extreme hatred toward Herod and Rome. They aimed their bitterness and anger at everything and everyone—even their family and friends. They could not find any peace. Vengeance and revenge seemed to consume and drive their every action—their every breath.

Dismas was one of them. The Dismas we knew as loving and peaceful, who would light up when Simon ran to him, was gone emotionally. Instead, Dismas seemed to spend every waking hour trying to figure out how to retaliate against Herod the Great and the Romans who put him in power. To Dismas, Herod and the Romans were one and the same. They jointly were responsible for Simon's death. Both were accountable for the oppression throughout the land. The brother that I knew and loved seemed to have died with Simon. Nothing we could do would bring him back. We lost Simon. I was afraid we had lost Dismas too. For many, Bethlehem was forever changed.

In short order, Dismas became a thief but stole only from those associated with the government and their close acquaintances. He was attempting to return the misery and hurt they had caused him. He was risking his life with each robbery and disturbance, but he did not care. His anger and his hate were all-consuming. Dismas was no longer a shepherd. He, like me, had tended the flocks when he was young. When he turned of age, Father taught him to be a stonemason, and they worked together every day. Father would do the same for me when I came of age. Father and

Dismas spent most of their time working in Bethlehem, Jerusalem, Herodium, or the surrounding villages. They often kept the aqueduct in good repair and watertight to keep the water flowing from Bethlehem to Jerusalem. They knew the land and the terrain of Judea well. Over time, Father would come home saying that Dismas did not show up or left at midday. When he did show up for work, his mind would be far away. Father worried that his son would get badly hurt from not paying attention when he did work. As days passed, Father found himself increasingly stranded and alone.

As the weeks passed, Dismas was less and less at home during the night. When he was home, he was sullen. His face was full of sadness and anger. He would spend hours staring into the distance, saying nothing, barely eating, moving little. He was like a stranger. We were so worried but at a loss as to how to help him. We tried doing things he liked, fixing his favorite foods, and reminding him of happier times; but nothing worked.

Before long, we noticed that his clothes and a few of his possessions had disappeared. Afterward, we heard that he had joined a small group of others from the region who had also lost brothers or cousins. All were filled with rage. We imagined that they would scheme what they could do next to harass, rob, or annoy all those linked to Herod. They were on a dangerous path.

Now and then, Dismas would show up at night after supper, saying he missed us and just wanted to see how we were doing. When here, he would hug Mother, and all would cry for Simon. Though we pleaded, he would not say what he was doing. We begged him to stop if the revenge rumors were true. We warned him that he could be seriously hurt or worse. Instead, he would just leave again—often without even saying goodbye—many times in midsentence.

Before long, weeks and months would go by with no word from him. About that time, we heard the news of bandits burning possessions of those linked with the government. These stories were followed by tales of robberies, frightening wives and children, defacing and destroying property, scattering horses, and more. Disruption and harm were now being inflicted on the government with an ever-increasing frequency. Surely, Dismas was a part of this unrest. We assumed that he and his friends were surviving by selling the items they stole. How else were they going to have food or clothing and, sadly, weapons? We never heard that the bandits included Dismas, but we knew.

I am sure that Dismas and his bandits worked hard to keep their identities and relationships with us unknown so as to protect us. If the Romans thought that Dismas was a relative of ours, the soldiers would have ruthlessly pressed and even harmed us to make us tell them where Dismas was hiding. If caught, the bandits' best hope was prison, followed by flogging. Thirty-nine lashes would await them. Forty lashes were believed to be the number needed to kill someone. So receiving thirty-nine lashes was the punishment required to bring the prisoner to within an inch of death but still keep him alive. Their very worst future would be death by crucifixion. To the citizens' belief, the Romans did not need a good excuse to crucify those they did not like.

Before long, news of destruction and turmoil came from villages and regions farther away from Bethlehem. Word of the attacks filtered to us from throughout the countryside. The rebellions ranged from Jerusalem to the small towns and villages further north, even into Galilee. The bandits surely realized that they needed to move to remain free while still causing their constant mischief. While this kept them better hidden from the authorities, it also meant that we did not know where they were.

Even though we heard of attacks in Jerusalem, one of our daily prayers was that Dismas and his gang would not go or return to Jerusalem. Jerusalem was a bustling city with the largest number of Romans and their affiliates—none of whom were exempt from Dismas's mayhem. In addition, Jerusalem had a constant flow of visitors and traders. Many came to visit the temple and participate in religious events. Others were traders, merchants, craftsmen, and government workers there to support the economy and its residents. Thus, politics, commerce, religion, military, family, and social activities made the city a constant hive of activity.

On the one hand, for bandits like Dismas, Jerusalem would be a relatively easy place to hide while also providing many opportunities for retaliation. On the other hand, the size of Herod's and Rome's military presence, in addition to a large number of citizens who would tell the Romans of their presence, made Jerusalem the most dangerous of places. In our minds, Jerusalem, by far, was the place of their greatest danger. So my daily prayer became, "Dear God, please keep Dismas out of harm's way and away from Jerusalem."

Trying to Understand
Hatred and Oppression

ONCE WHILE HOME FROM tending the flocks, my
father, Lucius, was also home from his building project in Herodium, south of Bethlehem.
Father's work was usually in Jerusalem, a half day's walk
north, or Herodium, only an hour or two south. Bethlehem
was great as a central location, enabling him to get home
more often than others whose work was farther away.
During one of those somewhat rare times when both he
and I were home together, I asked why Herod was so mean
and why he seemed so much like a Roman. Was he not
Jewish—just like us?

"Father," I added, "help me understand why he seems
to take so much of everything you and the others earn
and why his soldiers would do things like kill Simon and
Bethlehem's other young boys." Father started by saying
that what he was about to tell me was mainly learned from
stories passed down over time by fellow villagers and travelers passing through Judea.

He started by clarifying that Herod was not Jewish
by birth, saying, "Yes, he has the title 'King of the Jews'

as appointed to him by Emperor Augustus Caesar in Rome. Herod was born west of Jerusalem in an area called Idumean or Edom. Though Herod rules our nation, he was born and raised in a culture very different from ours. Many call him a half Jew. A century or so ago, King Hyrcanus conquered Jordan and forced its citizens to become Jewish. So Herod's ancestors had to become Jews. In turn, when Herod was born, he became Jewish. However, Herod, as he grew, decided that he did not want to be of our religion. He determined he would never follow our laws or practices. So, you see, he is called the 'King of the Jews' but has never believed or practiced our religion. He is Jewish in name only."

"But, Father, how did a Jordanian come to be the king of the Jews and rule us so strictly?"

Father shook his head, saying, "It is a long and sad story for our people. Herod's father was named Antipas. Antipas met Caesar and sided with him in battle. In appreciation, Caesar appointed Roman citizenship to Antipas. Antipas had two sons, Phasael and Herod, the latter who is now our king. In time, Phasael was granted governorship over Judea, and Herod was appointed governor of Galilee.

"As you grow, you will hear more about the assassination of Caesar. When a leader is murdered to overthrow and create a new government, that is called an assassination. Those spearheading the assassination would often kill the ruler to become the new leader—the new king. They did not care about the government or its citizens. They just wanted to assume power and become the new ruler. The killing of Caesar was terrible for us because Caesar was a good ruler in that he let us be Jewish. After Caesar's death, war broke out between those who had supported him and those who wanted to rule the new government. The war forced people, like Herod, to choose which side they would serve.

"The murderers of Caesar were Brutus and Cassius. They led the new regime. Mark Anthony led the supporters of Caesar on the other side. Herod and his father, Antipas, sided with the assassins Brutus and Cassius. Soon after, the murderous side started demanding large amounts of money to support their war effort. Cassius was so desperate for cash that he even declared that any leader not raising his share would be sold into slavery.

"Herod, who was always eager to please, was the first to meet his monetary goal. Raising funds from Galilee is difficult since the land is mainly farming and small villages. The region has no mines, factories, seaports, or any other major industry from which Herod could raise large amounts of taxes. His only tax source was from the poor farmers, fishermen, shepherds, merchants, and tradespeople, like me. But that did not stop Herod.

"As Herod levied new and continuously raised taxes, the people's hatred for him grew and grew. Bandits even formed to resist him. It got so bad that Rome eventually charged Herod with overstepping his legal authority. Rome called him to Italy to stand trial, but in the end, he was found innocent and freed. When he returned, he went to Damascus to live.

"Over time, Brutus and Cassius's side was defeated. Herod found himself now on the wrong side of the government. Phasael, Herod's brother, was captured and eventually killed. Frightened for their lives, Herod and his family escaped to Masada, southeast of us. In desperation, Herod left his family in Masada and reached out to Rome. His goal was to meet and bribe Mark Anthony and the Roman Senate. He needed to become an ally with the new ruling party. Herod must be one persuasive, smooth-talking diplomat because his appeal worked. His one-time and recent enemy, for some reason, accepted Herod and granted him Rome's favor.

"Once again in Rome's good graces, Herod started trying to convince Rome that its main enemy was the Parthians who had captured and killed his brother, Phasael. The Parthians had now even invaded Jerusalem. In response, the Roman Senate rewarded Herod by appointing him king of the Jews to rule Judea.

"As our new king, Rome granted Herod an army with orders to defeat and cast out the Parthians, then secure and stabilize the land. After roughly three years, Herod and his army finally won. Herod has now been the ruler of our land for thirty-three years, and for decades, we have lived under his control of Judea and his oppression."

Father continued, "Knowing that he was so hated, Herod tried some things to appease his Jewish citizens. Probably his most well-received act was refurbishing the temple. You see, Aaron, the temple in Jerusalem is actually our second temple. The first one, the one that Solomon built, was destroyed several centuries ago. The second temple—the one now being rebuilt, enlarged, and enhanced—

was started shortly after the first temple's destruction. But it was rather small and somewhat insignificant.

"Today's Jerusalem temple, while still being refurbished, is already magnificent. Its sanctuary is massive. The renovation will likely still take a few more decades before being finished. I have been fortunate to have worked on it several times. I have helped build and repair parts of its massive outdoor courtyard that can hold thousands upon thousands of worshipers. I have been able to work on the holy structure's gigantic walls and its many entrances. My work on the aqueducts has helped bring water to the temple grounds.

"Being built on the hill where God told Abraham to sacrifice his son, Isaac, the building requires massively thick and high walls to support its weight and the weight of its many believers who worship there. God has blessed me by allowing me to build his temple. My work there has been one of reverence and love. I pray God will give me more opportunities to construct the sanctuary for our worship. Knowing that my work will help provide a place for you, my family, and my fellow Jewish believers to draw near to God has been and is a true blessing. This temple will last for centuries upon centuries.

"The opportunity to help build the temple, along with Herod's many other building projects, was part of what encouraged me to become a stonemason. Hopefully, there will always be a need for this type of work. Plus, I will not have to deal with the worries of drought and famine that plague so many of our farmer neighbors. Soon you will be able to learn the trade and get to work with me! That day will be glorious! I am excited, Aaron. I hope you are too. It is a good, noble profession that will enable you to provide for your family. You will make an excellent stonemason. I am sure of it!"

After beaming and I am sure blushing, I asked, "Father, you said that Herod has done a few good things to make the Judeans happier with him. You mentioned his work on the temple. Are there others?"

"Aaron, you have heard your mother and me talk about graven images and how the images of people are forbidden from being displayed on items. In many lands, the ruling government issues coins and money adorned with the portraits of their emperor, king, governor, and prefects—whoever is their ruler. Like many of these, Herod could mint our money with his image or that of the Roman emperor. But knowing how much we, his citizens, hate that practice, Herod has chosen not to make money with anyone's face on it. That is a good thing.

"So, Father, Herod seems to respect our people to some degree with the reconstruction of the temple and not defacing our money. Why does he do things like having his soldiers kill babies like Simon?" Father immediately looked sad and dejected. He shook his head, saying, "Herod is a dictator—all-powerful with the backing of Rome. Herod has learned that he can do almost whatever he wants if he does not get into trouble with the Roman government.

"Much of the Jews' hatred of Herod originates from the many taxes he makes us pay. Each man in Judea pays three duties or taxes. First, as you know, this land, and what it produces, is God's. God placed us here to tend to and care for it. We give a tithe of one-tenth of whatever we produce back to God. We give that freely and joyfully. Secondly, we pay a temple tax to support the temple's operations. Those operations are run or managed by the Sadducees who live far too refined and easy in the eyes of hardworking citizens like me. My temple tax helps pay for their extravagance. I do not resent supporting the temple, but I resent the excess and waste I see from the religious leaders. So this second tax is our religious-based tax, but that is not all.

"We must also pay a governmental tax which is used to support not only Herod and his local government but also Rome. That is our penalty for being part of the Roman Empire. To us, it seems like when Herod needs more money for his lavish lifestyle, his many building projects, or whenever Rome needs more, he just adds new taxes and fees on items such as goods and services—the fruits of our labor. It never ends, and the people's resentment against him builds and builds.

"Herod's appetite for new building projects is insatiable. While he has restored the temple in Jerusalem, he has also built an amphitheater, a palace, a race hippodrome, and many more buildings that I cannot even remember. He has even created a brand-new Mediterranean port city named Caesarea. Its elaborate palace and massive, ornate shipping harbor are said to be the best in all the land.

"But, Aaron, the worst of his construction projects is his hated theater. Almost daily, the theater holds battles among lions, tigers, bears, and other dangerous animals. He also sponsors fights among humans, and they always lead to death. Sometimes, the matches are between men, but often a ferocious animal and a human must fight each other. Each battle ends the same. Either the man or animal dies—most often the man. The fights are brutal and all held just to entertain the paying customers watching from the stands. Can you believe people come to watch such horror? It shows that they do not respect us, nor do they value us as a people. Almost every Jewish citizen in the region knows of or has lost a friend, neighbor, or loved one this way. Horrible! Do you see why we hate Herod so?" All I could do was nod yes.

Shaking his head, he added, "And just wait 'til you see Herodium. You will not believe such ornateness, such extravagance. It is so pompous—the height of opulence. And all built from our taxes. On a clear day, you can see it on our southern horizon. It contains cisterns and baths— built on three levels. All that you see is not natural. Herod had a mountain built that was not originally there. Our king wanted to build a mountain, so he built a mountain. Everything you see on the horizon was built by man— mostly by slaves and conscripted contractors, like me. And to think, it is not finished. Herod just keeps thinking of something to add that will make his home even grander. Someday, when you become a tradesman working with me, I do not doubt that we will be conscripted to work there again. You will not believe what he has built.

"I've mentioned his palaces in Caesarea and Herodium. You know he has one in Jerusalem. Did you know that he also has palaces in Masada and Jericho? There may be more that I do not know about or remember. But one thing I know for certain is that the money to build his many homes, his ports, and his many sources of entertainment have all come from taxes on poor, hardworking citizens like me. Our taxes and our cheap labor, along with slave labor, build that lavishness!

"That, in part, is why so many families were discouraged at having to be counted in the census. With everyone counted and recorded, Herod and Rome can more easily find us and our households and ensure we are taxed. So, Aaron, yes, Herod is our oppressor. We are under his constant thumb! These hardships, in part, are why the Jewish people anxiously await its Messiah, its Christ. Indeed, your new friend, Jesus, will save us from our oppressors and those who inflict those burdens.

"You also asked why Herod came to Bethlehem and murdered our eighteen young boys. I wish we knew why. Unfortunately, murder is common practice with Herod. Do you know that he has murdered some of his own family? I have heard that he became suspicious of them and their intentions. The word is that he was afraid they would overthrow him as king and might even kill him. So what did he do? He killed them—his own family! If he does not mind killing his own kin, he will not give a second thought to killing our babies.

"Why he did what he did here in Bethlehem, and only here in Bethlehem, only he knows. It is a great mystery that we ask ourselves every day. None of the townspeople can imagine what anyone, or any group, did to cause such horror. Something obviously worried him. We figure that by killing our baby boys, he believes he has removed that threat. But what threat could be caused by infants? Maybe he wanted to make Bethlehem an example to remind the whole kingdom of his authority. Whatever the cause, his killing of our baby boys showed us his power and that we are not to challenge him. I wish I knew why he did what he did, but the citizen's hatred of him has risen to a point I have never seen before. Just look at Dismas. My prayer is that Dismas will be careful, that he will be safe, and that God will protect him. But most of all, I pray that God will remove his anger and return him to us. I am just afraid Dismas has gone too far to ever be able to come back to us. We need to go. It is about time for dinner."

The Holy Family in Egypt

And out of Egypt I called My son.
—Hosea 11:1 (NASB)

A FEW MONTHS LATER, more monumental events happened in our family's life. First, we learned that Herod had died and that the authorities were preparing an elaborate funeral for him at Herodium. Earlier in the year, I witnessed the birth of Jesus and the killing of Simon. Now later that same year, Herod died. Three significant events in one year made me sure this would be a year that I would never forget.

Immediately upon Herod's death, everyone started hoping that his death would change our lives for the better. At first, we were relieved and even rejoiced to be free of our "king of the Jews"! However, we soon started worrying about who would replace him as our new ruler. Surely, he could not be as bad as Herod. We were wrong.

A few months later, we received a letter from Dismas saying he was hiding in Egypt. He and his friends were worried that the soldiers had narrowed their search and were closing in on them. At least for a while, escaping to Egypt seemed like the safest thing to do. While in this new land, they stopped at a tent community outside of Heliopolis, near the city of Cairo. Though his letter did not say, we wondered if his bandits would start attacking the Romans and their friends located there since Egypt had recently become a part of the seemingly ever-growing Roman Empire.

One part of his letter especially caught my attention. As Dismas and his friends bided their time spending a few days with the other settlers, they came upon a young couple with a tiny baby sitting under a giant sycamore tree. Around the campfire that night, he learned their names were Joseph, his wife Mary, and their Son Jesus. Those names reminded him of my stories of a baby named Jesus being born in Bethlehem in a stable. That memory made him ask where Jesus had been born.

Joseph said Jesus had been born in Bethlehem a few months earlier during Caesar Augustus's call for a census. Dismas excitedly asked if a small group of shepherds had come the night of Jesus's birth to see them while in a stable. Joseph looked at Mary with amazement, smiled, and nodded, saying, "Yes, how did you know?"

Dismas responded, "Do you remember a young boy named Aaron who was with them and then came to see you and Jesus almost every day after that?"

Mary smiled. "Oh, yes! Aaron—how we have missed him. What a dear boy. Aaron's excitement when he came to see us filled the room. He so liked to hold Jesus. How do you know him? What can you tell us about him?"

Dismas wrote that he told Mary and Joseph that I was his little brother and that whenever I was around him and the family, all I could talk about was that starry night and the following days being with them. Dismas shared that one of his best memories was of my telling and retelling of the times I got to hold Jesus. Dismas added that Mary sat quietly around the fire, smiling—taking in these memories.

After a while, Mary turned and asked Dismas, "Would you like to hold Jesus as Aaron did?" Dismas wrote how special that moment was for him. He, too, marveled that this tiny baby was to grow and become our Savior. If the angel's foretellings come true, this little boy will change the world and all in it. He added that he could never imagine his Savior living in a tent in the desert, seeking shelter from the sun while under a tree. Dismas then asked what had brought them from Bethlehem to Egypt.

Joseph said that one night, while in Bethlehem, an angel came to him warning that his family was in danger and that they must flee to Egypt to avoid Herod's wrath. Further, the angel warned that Herod intended to kill Jesus. With these words, Dismas wrote that he thought back to my stories of the Holy Family's quick departure, and then, in the next few days, our family witnessed the aftermath of the soldiers' slaughter of Simon and the baby boys.

These memories brought him such great sadness. Mary noticed and asked if he was feeling well. With that, Dismas handed Jesus back to her, saying he was fine but had to go. With that, he left. He did not want to upset them by telling them what had happened in Bethlehem soon after they left. How sad they would be to realize that innocent children had probably been killed because of their son. As painful as it was, Simon's loss now made sense.

Herod wanted to eliminate his challenger—the new King of the Jews! Herod must have been threatened by Jesus and who he would become. Perhaps he knew the scriptures. Or maybe the magi asking in Jerusalem where to find the newborn King of the Jews caused Herod to come here and remove the threat to his throne. It was hard to fathom that a baby could be a threat to the all-powerful Herod. However, to Herod, the best and most common way to deal with a problem was to eliminate it. By killing all boys aged two and under, Herod would be confident the one that mattered most to him—his threat—would be eliminated. This logic was the only explanation that made any sense. Dismas wrote in large, strong letters, "I HATE HEROD! I HATE THE ROMANS! I WILL MAKE THEM ALL PAY!"

As Father struggled to read the letter, the room grew quiet. I heard my mother weeping and deep sighs coming from my Father. After a long while, he was able to finish. Thank goodness that Dismas's letter ended on a positive note. He wrote, "Aaron, you were right—Mary has the most loving and beautiful eyes that I, too, have ever seen. The family is safe. Jesus has wonderful parents. Don't worry about me."

Though the letter brought great sadness, I was finally able to understand the reason behind Simon's murder. It especially hurt to know that Simon's death and Jesus's birth were joined together. My great joy in Jesus's coming was tempered by knowing his coming led to my baby brother's death. Jesus's birth also became the root cause of my family's second loss—the loss of Dismas. I hated that the letter made my anger at Herod resurface and refresh my pain.

Herod was responsible for the loss of two of my brothers. Dismas's words of hatred confirmed that we would now see and hear from him even less. One part of the letter, however, gave me great relief. I now knew the Holy Family was safe.

A New Government

NOT LONG AFTER KING Herod's death, word came that his last will and testament declared that his massive kingdom was to be divided into three parcels—one to be governed by each of his three sons. In his lifetime and to our knowledge, Herod had had nine sons and five daughters. However, Herod had previously killed three of his sons. In his will, he declared that, of his remaining sons, Archelaus was to rule Judea—our land. Antipas, named after his grandfather, was to rule Galilee; and Phillip was to oversee the Gentiles in the Golan region. Regardless of Herod's wishes, with the kingdom being under Roman authority, Rome mandated that all governance throughout its empire must be approved by them, whether it be one region or three.

Before Rome ratified Herod's wishes, Archelaus commenced ruling as if he were now in charge. He knew the people hated his father. He swore to the Judeans that his own rule would be kinder and less oppressive. The Judeans took this as an opportunity to ask Archelaus to release the political prisoners whom Herod had arrested. They also asked to be freed from his father's oppressive taxation. Some even went so far as to ask that many of Herod's administrators be brought to justice. However, one request on which all citizens could agree was that Archelaus appoint a Jewish high priest as their spiritual leader, as opposed to a political appointee who primarily served as a governmental puppet.

What happened, however, was that the anger that had been building among the people throughout Herod's reign surfaced to overflowing. Trying to calm the unrest, Archelaus brought in a small band of soldiers to restore order. Instead, tensions continued to escalate. In response, Archelaus brought in an army during Passover. A bloodbath resulted, with most of the blood being shed on the temple's grounds. Thousands of innocent men, women, and children were killed. The fire of hatred was fanned to new heights.

When Rome heard of the unrest, Archelaus knew he needed to go there and plead his case that his father's wishes, his will, be honored. However, when he got to Rome, he was shocked to find that his brother Antipas was already there. Antipas was pleading that Herod's crown and entire region be given entirely to him.

Like his brother Archelaus in Judea, Antipas had started ruling Galilee as its king. His plans included a massive building program like his father's. Word filtered down to Judea that he had begun rebuilding Sepphoris, which I remember Joseph saying was just north of Nazareth. This was the city that had recently been destroyed. We heard that Herod Antipas, as he was called, wanted to rebuild Sepphoris as a planned city—a feat never before accomplished. He wanted it to be called the "ornament of Galilee." I often wondered if Joseph and Jesus would be conscripted to work on those governmental rebuilding projects as had Father and Dismas been forced to work on Herod's Jerusalem and Herodium projects.

Regardless, Archelaus and Antipas were simultaneously in Rome, each pleading with the government that he, and not his brother, be granted their father's entire region to rule. At least, they hoped to get their third.

While all of this was happening, another massacre at Jerusalem's temple occurred. In response, a group of civilian leaders went to Rome to plead that neither Archelaus nor Antipas be appointed king. Instead, they requested that Herod's land be annexed to Roman Syria so that Rome could govern the land. Their appeal had one main request—one plea: the Jews be to be able to live by their own laws and their own scripture.

Despite Jerusalem's massive bloodshed, the unrest, and the citizens' pleas, Emperor Augustus and the Roman Senate acknowledged King Herod's loyalty to Rome by agreeing to honor his request. Herod's loyalty to Rome prevailed. The land would be divided into three regions. Archelaus was appointed to rule Judea; Antipas—Galilee; and Phillip— the Gentile region. In addition, Rome declared that none of the three regions' new rulers were to be called kings. Thus, Archelaus became Judea's "ruler of the people." Would not Herod the Great be shocked to learn that there was now only one King of the Jews in Judea? His name—Jesus!

While Archelaus was away, many bands of soldiers formed. Competing factions of enraged young male citizens also banded together. In no time, Judea was being terrorized on multiple fronts. Some of the citizens focused on being bandits and creating havoc. Others wanted to form their own new government. What was horrendous was that these factions—Roman and civilians alike—had all become ruthless. Murder, rape, robbery, and arson spread across the land. Whole villages were burned to the ground. Among the worst of the atrocities was the selling of our citizens into slavery.

The people's dreaded angst following Herod's death proved to be true. In so many ways, life in the next few years following Jesus's birth and Herod's death was far worse than it had been under Herod. Who could have ever imagined things getting worse? That, however, is how we found life in those years. I could not wait for Jesus to save us from this turmoil and oppression. He is to be our Savior! I pledged in my prayers to help him do what I could to end this horror. Waiting until Jesus grew of age was going to be hard, but my hope in him and my anticipation of a new era were strong and powerful. My hope and optimism in Jesus sustained me during these dark days.

During the following wheat-and-barley-harvesting season, Dismas unexpectedly showed up one night at the house. He looked exhausted, and his clothes were threadbare. His eyes were hollow with no signs of life or joy. While he reminded us of the Dismas we knew and loved, his actions and personality were foreign to us. He asked about each of us, but he mainly seemed to do so because our parents had taught him manners. Mostly, he was distant.

I asked, and he talked about his visit with the Holy Family in Egypt. Unfortunately, the discussion made him remember Simon's killing. His talk turned quickly to his hatred of Herod's offspring and their Roman supporters. He stressed that something somehow must be done to get rid of them and get our land back. As we talked, I was consoled knowing that, though Jesus's birth had caused Simon's murder, it was not Jesus's fault. He was an innocent infant. The responsibility was all Herod's. Simon's loss did not lessen my love and hope for Jesus as he grew and became my Savior. I was so thankful I had these feelings. Dismas would not talk about it at all.

Then out of the blue, Dismas said he hoped in a decade or two that the Jesus we had both seen and held as a baby would rise to power and defeat our enemies. When that movement began, Dismas swore he would be among the first to join Jesus's army. He could not wait. "As a soldier in Jesus's army, I will finally be able to avenge Simon's death!" He was positive that he could recruit scores of men to fight for Jesus's cause. He said he often spent days dreaming of the day when Jesus would be declared King and Archelaus overthrown. For a moment, I saw the brother I had known before the murders—smiling, a gleam in his eyes, with hope and promise in his heart.

Maybe in ten to fifteen years, things would start to change. God would be in charge. Jesus would reveal himself to everyone. Our Savior would be worshiped and exalted by all his people, and all would rally around him. The Promised Land would finally be returned and restored to its people. Happiness would abound; pride would prevail. Peace, once again, would be known throughout the land. And our children would finally understand what the word *peace* truly means. People everywhere would know that God is with *us*—not them, *us*! We would not be threatened again. We had God and his Son on our side. We could not wait. And like that, Dismas was gone again—only to be heard from through people's stories and a few letters.

GROWING INTO MANHOOD

A S FOR ME, THE year I came of age, I started learning to be a stonemason, working by my father's side every day. Days were busy and so unlike the days of a shepherd. I now had to pay attention every minute of every day—no more daydreaming or stargazing for me. Not being focused could get you hurt. I found that my thinking about Jesus was now mainly limited to the evenings after supper.

I started a new ritual. Every night, I would recite the words of the angel, "Do not be afraid. I bring you good news of great joy which shall be for all the people, for today in the city of David there has been born for you a Savior, who is Christ the Lord. And this will be a sign for you: you will find a babe wrapped in swaddling clothes lying in a manger." I knew I did not want to forget those words. So repeating them every night was my best way to ensure that I would remember them forever.

When in bed, I often found myself wondering if Jesus now had new brothers and sisters and, as they grew, what they would think about living with the Christ. Would they comprehend what having their brother as their Savior meant, or would Mary and Joseph even tell them? Would they believe, or would they just scoff, saying, "He is no different from me or any other boy in the region! He hit his thumb the other day with the hammer and cried out in pain. Would our Savior do that?"

As Jesus grew, I wondered how well Mary and Joseph would cope with being the parents of the Son of God? When they were here, they worried whether they would be good parents and the parents God expected of them. Would they constantly question if they were doing a good job—the job God wanted? Would people notice any difference in Jesus from other boys and girls? School surely was in his future, living, and playing in and around other children—some shy, some bullies, some friends, some enemies. How would he deal with all these differences? If I were in school with him, would he seem like me, or would he be different in a way that I could not understand? Would he even mention his role; and if he did, would he be greeted with acceptance or with laughter, scorn, or accusation that he had gone mad? How would he deal with death and sickness? Would he be happy and sad like me?

At night, I constantly found myself asking God why he would let his Son be born in a manger? "You started him out in a lowly stable. Was life any better for them now, wherever he and his family now lived?" It seemed like each night I came up with new questions, new expectations, and new anticipations of when he was going to reveal himself. I especially wondered how Mary and Joseph were coping. Oh, how I missed them—especially Mary. I knew that they were out there somewhere, but I did not know where. Had they returned to Nazareth? Wherever they lived, would not

Jesus's fellow villagers be shocked to know who was living right there in their midst?

When I was fourteen and Jesus would have been four, I continued to learn my trade. I started taking on more and more of the role Dismas had served while helping Father. My strength increased greatly as I used my back, arms, and legs to lift and place heavy stones. My education was behind that of other boys my age since I had spent so much time with the flocks, but I caught up quickly. In the evenings, our father would teach my siblings and me. Being home almost every night gave us the time we needed to learn to read, write, and do math—all skills I needed in our trade. Through it all, I grew in stature, strength, and skill.

In my free time, I was able to go to the synagogue where the rabbis explained the scriptures, but mainly they helped us in our reading so we could better understand the scriptures on our own. Their teachings allowed me to learn more about our Jewish religion, the Torah, our heritage, and the many prophecies. My connection with Jesus made me hungry to learn about any prophecy that proclaimed the coming of our Savior, the Christ or the Messiah.

Over time, I came to love two ancient verses. One day, the priest read the words of the prophet Micah, who had said, "As for you Bethlehem, though you are small among the clans of Judea, out of you will come for me one who will be ruler over Israel." I knew the scriptures spoke of Bethlehem, but I thought the only references related to David or Ruth. Here, however, Micah prophesied, long after David and Ruth had lived, that a new ruler of Israel would come from my own hometown! When I heard those words for the first time, I got so excited that I shouted out loud, "That is true! It has happened! Four years ago, in Bethlehem. I saw the Holy Family. I even held our Savior! He is here already! His name is Jesus! He should be four years old now!"

Everyone turned to stare at me, asking, "Why do you say that?"

"Because I saw it. I was there! He is here! Our Christ has been born—right here in Bethlehem, just like Micah said. Micah was right. Jesus is in Judea somewhere. I do not know where, but I know he is here. I saw him!" Though doubters mostly filled the room, they still asked me to explain. I guess they were just too curious. I ended up telling them the whole story.

They learned of the star, the angels, our going to see Mary and Joseph, and our finding Jesus lying in the manger—at a house just right down the road. I told them of holding Jesus and my many visits. I told them of the elderly Simeon and Anna and the visit from the royal and learned magi. I told them about Elizabeth, Zacharias, and John. Some agreed, saying that they had heard of Zacharias having a son in his old age.

Some were open to what I was saying, wanting to know more. Some scoffed, saying that God's son would never be born in a stable and that an insignificant shepherd boy would never get to hold their Savior—not their Christ! Most said that they had lived in Bethlehem for most of their lives and especially for the past four years. Why didn't they see the star? Why didn't they hear the angels sing or see their bright light? If God's Son had been born here, would not the religious leaders of the village be the first to know?

Several did acknowledge being puzzled as to why the magi had come, set up camp outside of town, and come to see a visiting family with their new baby. When I told them why Herod and his soldiers had murdered all of our baby boys, most nodded, saying that made sense. It didn't take much for Herod to be ruthless. Some were obviously going to think a lot about what I said long after I left. However, to others, what I said was so foreign to their beliefs they would never believe me. Finally, after rounds of bickering and growing weary, I finally told them they could believe what they wanted. I knew it to be true. I had seen him with my own eyes because I was there. I had touched God's Son. I was part of his revelation. They should rejoice!

The second ancient verse that resonated with me was a verse from the prophet Isaiah. Isaiah had lived in nearby Jerusalem. He, too, prophesied centuries before, saying, "For unto us a child is born, to us a son is given, and the government will be on his shoulders. And he will be called Wonderful Counselor, Mighty God, Everlasting Father, Prince of Peace." I spent hours thinking about those words. I knew that Jesus had already been born and was growing to be the good news the angels had announced. Isaiah's prophecy was underway. When Jesus becomes a man, he will be called wonderful, mighty, and everlasting. That part was easy to understand.

I struggled, however, with the words "Prince of Peace." "Prince"—I could understand. I was confident that he would be regal. The word *peace* was more challenging.

Maybe he would be the Prince of Peace after he overthrew the oppressive government. Conquering that powerful a force, however, could not be peaceful! Perhaps after he and we prevailed, his kingdom with its regions of Judea, Galilee, Samaria, and beyond would finally know peace. Then and only then could I imagine Jesus being known as "the Prince of Peace." A lot of nonpeaceful times would most likely precede any times of peace. I could not imagine Jesus being King any other way.

Imagining that peace could be achieved presented a whole new set of questions that I asked over and over. How on earth was Jesus going to defeat mighty Rome? Would he need to call down the heavens to win the battle? If not, and he had to rely solely on people like Dismas and me, victory seemed impossible. I just could not fathom the citizens forming a force large and strong enough to overthrow Antipas and his legions of support. I did not doubt that Rome would respond, if needed, by sending in all necessary resources to squash any rebellion. The main word that I kept saying was, "Impossible!"

During my sixteenth year, when Jesus would have been six, Father was injured and had to stay at home for many months recovering. He had broken his arm and leg and been badly cut when some stones he was securing high overhead shifted and fell on him, causing him to fall off the scaffolding and then have the stones fall on him. We were building a new home for a local newlywed couple. To build a house in our villages, we would take rocks and stack them one upon another. We held the rocks and stones in place with mortar made of mud, sand, and gravel. When the mortar dried, we would cover the walls with clay. After we finished, carpenters would come in, frame, make the doors, and build the roof supports for the house. People of our trade were often getting cut and bruised. However, Father's injury was the worst any in the family or village could remember. During his recovery, I did all I could to handle his workload and mine. Still, I was only sixteen and nowhere able to fulfill both duties, especially lifting the stones that he and I usually raised together. However, we needed the money to support the family and keep the soldiers at bay lest we not have enough to pay our taxes. Times were rough, but we made it through.

During my seventeenth through nineteenth years, when Jesus would have grown to be nine, Father had healed and was almost his old self. He walked with a limp for a while, but he was still very strong. Our new jobs took us more often to Jerusalem and Herodium. Though Herod had died, our new ruler, Archelaus, maintained the lavish lifestyle of his father, often vacationing at Herodium. That massive palace with its gardens, pools, and aqueducts was constantly in need of repair. If not needed for repairs, we could always count on being required to work on the constant expansions of the palace's walls, bridges, arches, courtyards, and spas. Work on the temple, the ruler's many projects, the constant needs for the aqueduct, and the pressing needs in our nearby villages meant that the skills of tradespeople, like us, were always in demand.

Getting paid was another story. Fellow citizens mostly paid by bartering goods and services. We did receive some money for our services; but we mostly were paid with animals, fish, fruits, and vegetables or with goods made by our customers. Instead of money, we were usually offered bread, pottery, cloth, sandals, furniture, leather goods, and the like in place of cash. Getting paid by the government, on the other hand, was always challenging and never timely, but it was always in cash.

In my twentieth or twenty-first year, when Jesus would have been ten or eleven, a group of Judeans went to Rome asking that Archelaus be removed as their "ruler of the people." Archelaus was a poor leader. Rome finally agreed and annexed our land as a Roman possession. However, Rome thought so little of Judea that they declared that the land become a Roman province governed by a prefect, Coponius, who reported to Syria. Despite our hopes and the victory of removing Archelaus, life did not change. Our government was different, but the same lifestyle remained. Over time, Prefect Coponius became our governor.

Lost in Jerusalem

And His parents used to go to Jerusalem every year at
the Feast of the Passover. And when He became twelve,
they went up there according to the custom of the Feast.
—Luke 2:41–42 (NASB)

TWELVE YEARS AFTER THE angels told us about Jesus's
birth, I was twenty-two and Jesus twelve. Passover
was approaching. All Jewish men who were able
to do so were required to go to Jerusalem to celebrate the
Passover holiday. I was going to celebrate and worship, but
also for another reason. The herdsmen of the sheep I had
once watched needed help getting the lambs to Jerusalem
for sacrifice. Two of their herdsmen were unable to go
because of illness or injuries. Plus, Passover was our most
sacred holiday and always drew the largest crowds, which
meant the need for more sacrificial animals. The extra load
plus the absences called for more help. I offered to assist.
After delivering the sheep to the temple authorities, we
joined the other commoners in worship. The Passover took
days upon days to celebrate. As we expected, the crowds
filled the city to overflowing.

The focus of our activities was to remember the Passover during Israel's captivity in Egypt. Moses, the Jewish leader, had foretold the Egyptian Pharaoh that a sequence of ten plagues would befall his people if he did not free the Hebrew people. When the Pharaoh failed to listen, the plagues started—one after another, causing all degrees of harm and pain to the Egyptians. Each plague was more severe than the one before. Despite these hardships, the Pharaoh continued to refuse to let our people go.

The last of the plagues was the Passover. On that Passover evening centuries ago, God allowed a household's firstborn to live if the home's residents marked the doorframe—its lintel—with the blood of a sacrificed lamb. The markings instructed the death angel to pass over these homes and spare all within.

For the homes with no lamb's blood on the lintel, the angel of death would kill the firstborn of that home's family. So that night, all of the Jewish families who obeyed the instructions were passed over. However, all Egyptian families who failed to place the blood on their door lost their firstborn child. After this last and most devastating plague, the Egyptian ruler finally became convinced that he could not defeat the God of Moses and his people. So, after decades of keeping the Jewish people in captivity and slavery, the Pharaoh reluctantly let them go. Free at last, with Moses as the lead, our ancestors headed for the Promised Land—our homeland.

That first Passover, God further instructed his people to eat an evening's meal of sacrificed lamb, along with bitter herbs and bread made without yeast. The people were to devour the meal quickly while fully clothed. When finished, the followers were to burn any portion of the meal that remained. God commanded his people to observe this remembrance and celebration every year. So, you see, celebrating Passover is our most important Jewish holiday. It is why we gather in the Holy City each year to celebrate the freedom that God bestowed on his chosen people.

However, not everything was peaceful or focused at that year's Passover celebration. Skirmishes with the Roman soldiers were erupting everywhere. Stories of stealing, property destruction, arson, and harassment toward those not Jewish swirled amongst us with increasing frequency. I could not help wondering if Dismas was involved in this chaos. Was he the leader of these bands or just one of the pack? I prayed for him constantly that he would be safe and come back to us soon. I so longed to have the Dismas we once knew and loved return to us. However, deep down in my heart, I knew that my prayers would never be answered the way I wanted.

After the Feast of the Passover celebration, the worshipers left to return home. The city cleared quickly. Because of our shepherdly duties, we stayed in the city a few extra days to retrieve the sheep and lambs that had not been sacrificed and ready them for the return back to the fields. Often, we had to remain longer just to get paid. We hoped and prayed that this year we would not have any hassles getting our funds.

While waiting in the Jerusalem streets, I heard the frantic cries of a man and woman yelling, "Jesus, Jesus—where are you?" Over and over, they shouted the name.

I rushed to the sound of the voices to see if I could help. When I found them and was about to shout, "Can I help?" the woman turned to look at me. In her eyes, I saw her desperation and her fear. Her eyes said it all. Standing before me was Mary—Jesus's mother. Yes, she was older, as was I; but she was the young mother I remembered! However, this time, she had the stricken look of worry and panic.

As gently as I could, I said, "Mary. Mary. It is me— Aaron. What is wrong? How can I help?"

As Joseph rushed over to join us, Mary, with a big sigh of anguish, cried out, "Aaron, Jesus is missing. We have not seen him for over two full days. We do not know where he is. Please help us find him?"

I asked, "How did this happen?"

Joseph jumped in, saying, "After Passover, we left with the others, heading back to our home in Nazareth. After traveling for a full day, we stopped to set up camp for the night. That is when we first missed Jesus. We looked everywhere. We started by going to our relatives and friends, but Jesus was not with any of them. We then went to nearby camps to see if he was there. Since then, we have been retracing our steps, looking everywhere, and asking everyone we met if they have seen him. We have just gotten back to Jerusalem, hoping to find him here. Jerusalem is the last place we saw him. We are now on our third day without him. Surely, he is somewhere here in the Holy City. We do not know where else to look!"

I said, "I am here. I will help you find him. Let us spread out and meet back here and then do it again and again, going to other places until we find him. I know we will find him. I know we will! Try not to worry!" All nodded, turned, and headed out in different directions calling for Jesus. I first rushed to the shepherds to tell them to proceed without me, saying I would join them once we found Jesus.

After five regatherings, Joseph, Mary, and I decided to go into the vast temple courtyard and look there. As we entered, we found several rabbis sitting on the temple's steps huddled around a young boy. When Mary saw them and the focus of their attention, she yelled to Joseph, "There he is!" With that, Mary, Joseph, and I rushed to them. As we drew closer, I stayed back but was still close enough to hear. Mary cried, "Jesus! Oh, my Son! Your father and I have been so frightened. We have been looking for you for days. Why have you treated us this way?"

Jesus stood amid the rabbis and said, "But, Mother, why were you looking for me? Did you not know that I would be about my Father's business in my Father's house?"

Mary and Joseph looked at each other, confused and bewildered. After a moment, they turned back to Jesus, saying, "Come, we must go back to Nazareth and not have you bother these fine temple leaders any longer."

With that, Jesus started moving toward Mary and Joseph, but before he left, one of the rabbis stood, saying, "Madam, your Son is most gifted. For the past two days, he has listened intently to our words and our teachings. He has asked questions. His understanding of the Torah and Jewish law is astonishing, especially for such a young boy. He is wise beyond his years. We, in turn, have asked him questions, and his answers show a remarkable insight into God's word, God's nature, and God's love and hope for his chosen people. We are sorry that his being with us has frightened you as you did not know where he was, but we have learned from him, and we hope he has learned from us. He is a gift from God! Go in peace. God bless you."

As the Holy Family left the courtyard, I joined them but trailed behind. Mary was crying tears of relief, joy, and thanksgiving. As we left the temple grounds, Mary stopped and hugged Jesus with tears of joy. I could see the worry evaporate from Mary's and Joseph's faces. I could see in Jesus's face his expression of appreciation for their love and care and also his concern that he had caused them such angst. After walking a block or two further through the city, Mary turned Jesus to face me, saying, "Aaron, forgive me. Jesus, I want you to meet someone you've met before but will not remember. This is Aaron. When you were born in Bethlehem, an angel appeared to Aaron and his fellow shepherds and told them about you and your birth. The angel told them to come to see us, and they did. When Aaron saw you, he was so excited. He asked if he could hold you. I put you in his arms, and he just smiled and rocked you back and forth. He was one of the first to hold you. Then almost every day we stayed in Bethlehem, Aaron came to see, hold, and play with you. Aaron was your first friend. Say hello to Aaron."

With that, Jesus looked at me and said, "Aaron, you are my brother. Thank you for being with my mother and father then and for helping them today. You are special. God is with you. Bless you." I nodded sheepishly, saying that it was my honor. I honestly did not know what to say. My Savior was talking to me. What do you say to your

Savior? All these years later, thinking back on that memorable day, I wish so badly that I had said more and gotten to know him better. I guess I was just overwhelmed and tongue-tied. He was standing within arm's length of me, smiling, and looking directly into my eyes. What do you say to your Savior?

About that time, we reached the outskirts of Jerusalem. The Holy Family turned north toward Nazareth as I turned south toward Bethlehem. I needed to reconnect with my fellow shepherds and the remnants of our flock. But oh, how I wish we could have just stopped and sat and let me find out more about them. After fond goodbyes, I watched until they were out of sight as they headed up the dirt road. As I walked back, I smiled, knowing that they were doing well and living in Nazareth. I had gotten to see Jesus as a young boy, witness his spiritual gifts, hear him talk, and be with him. I imagined that God was as happy as I was with the kind of young man Jesus was becoming. I beamed when I remembered my Christ telling me that God was with me. I will always cherish those first words to me from God's son.

As I had now grown accustomed to doing, I started wondering about so many more things. Jesus, you know your heavenly Father and was in his house—the temple. Does that mean you know you are the Christ and our Savior? I found myself amazed that our future leader looked and acted like every other young boy I had ever known. If you saw Jesus with his mother and father in a group of people anywhere, you would never pick him or them out as the Holy Family destined to fulfill God's plan. They were as normal as anyone you would ever meet.

More importantly, I wanted to ask him, "When will you reveal that you are the one? When can we experience the joy of having our Savior in our midst, leading us and making our lives better? From what will you save us— oppression, sickness, hatred, everything, what? Do you have a timetable for when you reveal your destiny, or will it just happen? Are you in touch with your cousin John? Do you talk to him about what's to come?" Despite my new growing list of questions, there was one thing of which I was confident. Surely, God led me here today to be in Jerusalem, help the Holy Family, and see the young boy I once held as a baby. God led me to the temple just as he had led Simeon and Anna to this same place those many years ago. This was no coincidence!

MARRIAGE

WHEN I WAS TWENTY-THREE and Jesus thirteen, life was pretty much like other years. We still did not know where Dismas lived or what he was doing. We still heard of bandits tormenting the Romans. Word started spreading about a new leader of the antagonists—a man named Barabbas. His notoriety was growing throughout the land. The word was that he was the leader behind an escalating number of attacks, robberies, arsons, and vandalism. All of this chaos was focused on harming those in power and any who found favor with them. The rumors were that Barabbas had Roman blood on his hands from recent murders. We wondered if they were indeed rumors or if this was the truth. While the groups that we assumed included Dismas were most often called bandits, Barabbas was most often called a rebel and a criminal. He was earning these titles, not just from the Romans but from everyone. All were afraid of him, citizens and officials alike. His anger had often gotten so out of hand that he even harmed Jewish citizens. His ruthlessness seemed to grow with each new story that drifted our way. He was taking the provocation of the authorities to a whole new level. If you were in his way, you were in danger no matter who you were.

When I turned twenty-four and Jesus fourteen, life changed dramatically for me. During this year, I let my parents know that I was interested in a beautiful teenage girl from the other side of Bethlehem. Her name was Hannah. With both of us coming from such a small village as Bethlehem, I had seen Hannah from afar for years. I had seen her at the well once or twice and walking the streets a few times. However, our first true, actual meeting was during the wedding feast of my families' friends.

Hannah was huddled with other girls while I huddled with young men my age. I kept looking over at her; and once she caught my eye, she turned away, blushing and shyly bowing her head. Throughout the celebration and dinner, I found myself constantly looking at her to the point my friends asked why I was so distracted. I finally asked if anyone knew that girl's name over there. A few said that her name was Hannah and her parents lived in the southwestern part of town. They told me her father was a baker, adding that we were probably eating some of his bread today. As the evening went on, I got the nerve and went over to her, saying, "Hello, my name is Aaron. I hope you are having a good time at the wedding."

She replied, "Hello, Aaron, my name is Hannah. The wedding is quite special. Are you a friend or family member of the bride or the groom?" And that started it all. After our initial shyness, we started laughing and sharing our stories. What a glorious, magic-filled evening that was! I knew I had met the love of my life. I hoped she felt the same.

Not long after, I went to Mother and Father telling them that I had met Hannah and shared the excitement I had felt since meeting her. Father asked if I wanted to marry her and if he should go talk to her father to start the marriage negotiations. I said yes!

Our betrothal and marriage were somewhat unique compared to other Jewish nuptials. Most Jewish weddings were arranged by the parents, with the wedding couple often never having met each other until the wedding day. Hannah and I were fortunate to have met, even if only a few times. I think we met or saw each other three more times before being wed. With Bethlehem being such a small village, it was not that hard to run into each other while going about our daily lives.

Marriage in Judea was more than just the joining of man and wife; each family became relatives to the other. The couple's fathers would negotiate to ensure that the families were compatible and that a long-term bond would hold. For example, my father would negotiate the bride-wealth or bride-price—the price our family would offer to Hannah's family to help compensate for their loss of a productive young lady. The bride-price also showed her family my love for their daughter. The price offered by my family would help provide for Hannah in case something happened to me. If Hannah became a widow and our children fatherless, the bride-price would help support them. In turn, Hannah's father would negotiate the dowry that her family would offer us since Hannah would become my family's responsibility. Dowries often included land, goats, sheep, and chickens—items we needed and could use to sustain our new home.

Father and Mother were pleased with my choice, saying that Hannah was from a good family. They knew of Hannah's parents and especially of the father's bakery. When the wind was just right, the whole village knew Hannah's father was baking bread. Bethlehem smelled so wonderful during those days. The townsfolk could often be heard saying how they wished the wind would shift so that they could smell the aromas of his freshly baked bread.

Within the week, Father left to start the negotiations with Hannah's father. Upon his return, he would report on his progress. I was incredibly excited to hear what he learned of Hannah. Father reported that Hannah was skilled at cooking, washing, and making cloth on the loom. She was experienced in working the fields and orchards. But more importantly, her mother praised her for her goodness and gentleness in helping care for her younger brothers and sisters. She had a genuine loving spirit with a ready, warm smile. Like Mary, she, too, had loving eyes. Father added, "Aaron, the depth of Mary's eyes that has so captivated you is shared by Hannah."

I answered, "Yes, Father, I know. That tenderness was one of the first things that drew me to her."

Father added, "Hannah's father told me that she happily helps take care of the animals." After all those years of herding sheep, I knew all about what that required. Father took me by the shoulders and looked directly at me, proclaiming, "Aaron, you are a lucky man. Hannah is a lovely, loving, hardworking, warm, and tender young lady. She will make you a wonderful wife and will be the best of mothers to your children. Plus, you will have a wife who has learned to knead and bake bread from one of the very best bakers in all the land. You will eat well." Pulling out a loaf of her father's bread that he brought back with him, laughing, he added, "We hope to eat with you often!"

I know Father got tired of my asking how much longer he thought would be needed before the negotiations were final. He repeatedly smiled, saying, "Be patient. son. We are getting close. Probably only one or two more meetings." Within a few weeks, Father returned from meeting with her father, beaming, "Congratulations, Aaron. We have a marriage contract—you are betrothed! Next is your wedding, when you and Hannah will become man and wife!"

Mother jumped up and hugged me tightly, saying, "We have to start planning a wedding. There is so much to do!" I was so excited.

With the betrothal, Hannah and I were now legally husband and wife. However, she would live with her family and me with mine until the wedding. My main duty, before the wedding, was to prepare the wedding chamber. The chamber, a room to be added to my parents' home, would be my handiwork—my responsibility. The chamber, however, would not be completed until Father said it was ready. He was the final authority. I worked every night and every spare minute when our stonemason duties were not calling. I was fortunate that my trade was a real advantage. I was proud that I knew masonry and could build a sound, ample, weatherproof home for us. I would do all that I could to make Hannah proud of her new home and happy to be my wife.

At times, our betrothal year seemed to last forever; and then, at other times, it seemed to be upon us before we knew it. Weddings are the grandest celebrations most of us will ever witness. Everyone dresses in their best clothes, adornments, and sandals. Our wedding was to be in autumn. Then the weather was cooler, the crops gathered, the sheep sheared, the vineyards harvested. Autumn is the perfect time for a wedding—the perfect time for family and friends to celebrate and stay up later and longer than usual. Our wedding would be a time when all those who gathered to celebrate could drink a little more wine than they usually do while not having to worry so much about tomorrow's demands. It was a joyous time when the only thoughts were on celebrating the hopes and happiness of marriage—a time when all the toils and anxieties of daily life could subside.

Shortly after summer's end and upon my father declaring that the bedchamber was ready, I dressed in my finest and donned a crown of laurel branches. We called my groomsmen and my immediate family together. It was time to go and get my bride. As darkness started to fall, we headed to Hannah's house, with my groomsmen carrying torches lighting our way. I, the groom, followed. When we neared Hannah's house, I was to blow the trumpet and shout, announcing my coming for my bride. I was so surprised at how nervous I was. After a few feeble attempts and the encouragement of my groomsmen, the trumpet finally sounded loud and powerful.

Since the beginning of our betrothal, Hannah was to always be prepared for my arrival. She was not to know when I was coming but was to be always ready. So when she heard the horn and my shout, she dropped what she was doing, redressed, hurriedly gathered her things, and brought them to the door. As we waited, Hannah's father welcomed me into the family.

When Hannah arrived, she looked so beautiful. Her dress was perfect. I took her hand and looked into her eyes, saying, "Hannah, today I take you as my wife in accordance with the law of Moses and that of Israel." Upon my proclamation, my father started clapping. In a moment, everyone was clapping, shouting with excitement, and pressing around—all expressing their best wishes for us. After the greetings, Hannah's father said so that all could hear, "Aaron, my son, lead us to your house for the wedding and feast." With that, I took Hannah's hand and helped place her in a litter that my groomsmen would carry back to my house. The torchbearers, bridesmaids, and groomsmen led our procession, followed by the rest of the wedding party. As we walked down the streets, villagers rushed from their houses or hung from their windows, clapping and yelling encouragement. Many sang wedding songs. It was glorious! We looked forward to seeing them later, after the wedding, when they would join us for the festivities.

Upon entering the house, my parents blessed us by reading scripture. Hannah and I took our place at the table, and I hoisted a glass of wine, welcoming everyone and thanking them for being a part of this most glorious day. I took a sip, turned, and handed the glass to Hannah for her to drink. As she finished, the crowd yelled their hurrahs that I am sure were heard throughout Bethlehem. After a prayer, I enjoyed the music, dancing, games, and merriment while Hannah left with her bridesmaids and friends for her ritual cleansing.

The next day was the wedding ceremony. Hannah, dressed in white, joined the rabbi and me under the canopy, where he recited the blessings. Of the seven blessings, the one that meant the most to me read, "Let the loving couple be very happy, just as you made your creation happy in the garden of Eden, so long ago. You are blessed, Lord, who makes the bridegroom and the bride happy." When the rabbi finished, Hannah and I drank wine again, and with that, we were officially man and wife.

Along with our friends and family from miles around, the entire village joined the marriage feast. Spread before us was a feast of olives, dates, figs, grapes, cheese, nuts, fish, lamb, goat, and loaves of bread—the latter from Hannah's father's bakery. Smoked meats were a rarity in our household. They were so expensive, but today called for smoked meats. Huge barrels of wine were waiting for all. Hannah and I spent the day getting to know everyone who came. Many were from Hannah's family whom I had never met, and many from mine she had never met. At the end of the day, the feast was served separately to the men and women. During this time, our guests presented us with wonderful gifts. The festivities went on for days. The dancing, eating, and drinking never stopped. I cannot imagine a more perfect wedding, a more beautiful bride, or a more wonderful celebration with such loving families and friends. Well, that is not entirely true. If Dismas had been there, my wedding would have been all that I could have ever hoped to have. Regardless, I was blessed.

In time, everyone went home, and Hannah and I went about starting our new life together. Though we were getting used to each other with our new habits and routines, marriage life came easy for us. We were very happy. Hannah was the perfect wife. She became an instant, integral part of the household, loved by all. We visited her family as often as possible, and they welcomed me as their son. My family was happy for us to visit them since we never left without bringing back freshly baked bread—always enough for the whole family.

Hannah joined in helping with the chores and wished me well as I left each day to ply my trade. A new excitement filled my life. Each evening, I looked forward to returning home to her warmth, her smile, and her embrace. I dreamed of looking into her eyes each day. In her, I found such peace and love. Bethlehem had warmly welcomed its newest couple—Aaron and Hannah. Except for the government and military presence, life was all we could have hoped for.

WHERE IS JESUS?

DURING OUR FIRST WEEKS of marriage, one of my great joys was to tell Hannah my story of witnessing Jesus's first hours and the passing days. She had heard the hope of a coming Savior through her family or when she visited the synagogue, but to listen to my firsthand account brought forth a new sense of wonder and astonishment for her. I must have told her the story a dozen times, with her asking new thoughtful questions each time.

Before long, she had the same wonders as I. She, too, asked why the angels came to a few shepherds out in the field versus to the people right here in the village. She was in Bethlehem that night, but she and her family had not seen or heard anything out of the ordinary. They especially had not witnessed an exceedingly bright overhead star focused on her village. No commotion from angels had awakened them during the night. The following day, no one asked her or her family what all the racket was about last night. No one sensed anything unusual. So why announce only to a handful of shepherds? I could only shrug, chuckle, and tell her I had no idea but was so glad it happened and that it happened to me. Best of all, she believed me.

She, too, wondered why Jesus was born in a stable and laid in a manger. Again, I told her that I did not know but that I would take her to that house with its stable and manger if she wanted to go. It was only on the other side of the village. Not too far away at all. She, too, could see how lowly, how humble a setting that was. She would see that today it was just like it was then—another stable like all the others she had ever seen, with farm animals, hay, troughs, and animal smells. I told her that I wondered if she would be as amazed as I was and still am as she tried to comprehend that from such an ordinary, everyday setting, our wonderful counselor, our prince of peace, had been born. I told her to prepare herself.

When we arrived, I told her to imagine that right there, on that very spot, the words of the scriptures—the words prophesized from centuries and centuries ago—had been fulfilled. The words predicting that out of Bethlehem would come our Savior had, indeed, come true—right there. I hugged Hannah and said, "Hannah, I got to witness it all! I was there. It happened just as the prophets said—right there on that spot, right here in Bethlehem! Can you believe it?" Hannah laughed, seeing how very excited I was! I could not help myself. I found myself laughing, too, waving my arms, spinning around, and asking, "Can you believe it? Our Savior was born right here, lying in that very water trough, in this very cave, around animals like these, here in our hometown, not that far at all from our own home! Who could have imagined our Savior coming like that? I still cannot believe it! Yet I was here and got to see it all! I even held him! I held our Christ. Hannah, this is beyond wonderful!" I am not sure a day has gone by that I have not reflected on that starry night and all that happened to me. I know every day I smile, thanking God that I was a part of it. That night changed my life, and now it was changing Hannah's too.

Over the days and weeks, Hannah had new questions seemingly every day like the ones I had been having for years. One question she asked over and over was this: When would the day come that the nation could rejoice, knowing that God's plan of having Jesus as our King had begun? Unfortunately, I did not have answers for her. So I did what I do best when thinking about Jesus—I mostly just shrug and shake my head, saying, "I do not know. I wish I did."

It thrilled me to see that she believed me and was not doubtful, as were so many others. It was great to have someone share my excitement. We both constantly asked ourselves what it all meant, wondering when the proclamations and prophecies would come to be. Hannah said, "Jesus would now be fourteen. Surely, the time is getting close at hand. Do you think there will be a place for us in His Kingdom?" All I could say was, "I sure hope so." I understood so little.

By the end of my twenty-fifth year, when Jesus would have been fifteen, Hannah and I had moved into our own new home with a few animals and a few acres of land for crops, fruit trees, and a small vineyard. She was pregnant with our first child, and we spent every free moment getting ready for our new arrival.

In the next five years, when I turned thirty, and Jesus would have been twenty, life had given us its blessings and its sorrows. At twenty, Jesus would be a grown man. Most men his age would be fully into their careers, their calling, and many would have started their own families. Surely, I thought we would have heard about Jesus by now. Surely, we will hear from him soon.

By then, Hannah and I had two children—a boy, Daniel, now five, and a daughter, Rachel, now three. Father caught a fever and, after suffering through a long illness, died during the year. Our houses were devastated. I was distraught. Mother was despondent for weeks as she grieved. In my father, a finer man I have never known or met. I took over his work as best as I could but never felt that I measured up to being the man he was. He had been such a good father, provider, friend, workman, and the best grandfather ever.

Over this period, we heard from Dismas only once or twice and only through letters. He never came by—not for the funeral, not even in the dark of night. He had not met my wife or my children. Mother missed him terribly. I guess coming to his hometown just put all of us at too much risk.

We kept hearing stories of the soldiers capturing bands of bandits—never knowing if Dismas was with them or not. As seldom as they were, getting a letter from him was a great relief because they told us that he was alive and well. We were hearing of so many citizens being caught and crucified by the Romans. Major wrongs committed against society or the authorities seemed to quickly lead to one's crucifixion. However, the government seemed to crucify others simply because they did not like them. The charges against these prisoners often held little merit. Those indiscretions would not warrant death by crucifixion in a just society, but here in Judea, it did not matter—everyone was at the mercy of the authorities.

After all these years, I still hoped and prayed that Dismas's anger would leave him so that he could live an honorable life near us. I dreamed that he could join me, as he had father, as a stonemason. But I wondered, if his anger were to leave him, would he even be able to return? How well-known was he to the authorities? Did they know his name or just some descriptions that they had heard from others? One good thing—I had not seen his likeness nailed to posts or doorframes as I had seen for the hated Barabbas. If the government knew anything about him, he would always be a wanted man in their eyes, whether reformed or not. So the likelihood we could ever welcome Dismas back into our daily lives was remote. That thought just made his absence harder to endure.

During these five years, we heard nothing about or from Jesus. Quite frankly, I, unfortunately, found myself remembering less and less about that beautiful scene in the stable with the Holy Family. Two decades—twenty years— had passed, and nothing had happened on that front. A lot was happening in my life. Daily obligations took over my thoughts and attention. Twenty years is a long time to wait for anything to happen. Surely by the time Jesus had turned twenty, we would have heard something from or about him. Instead, nothing.

I had thought about traveling to Nazareth to look for the Holy Family and see how they were faring. However, I did not know if they even still lived there. Jesus very likely would have moved. It was a week's journey to Nazareth and then another week back. I just could not leave my family or my work for that long. I also expected to hear about John—the son of Elizabeth and Zacharias. He was to start telling people to get ready for the chosen one. Indeed, we would hear from John first. Two decades and nothing from either one of them. It was not only bewildering but also getting frustrating.

Though the awe and splendor of that first night still excite me, I must admit that I wondered more and more if anything was to come from what I had seen and heard. Had God's plans changed? Had Jesus and John done something to disappoint God to the point that the proclamations from the angels to such a small group in a remote field would just evaporate? So very few believed us, anyway. Of the shepherds with me, all but my cousin, who was a few years older than me, had died. While they lived, they were as excited as I was about that starry night. They wondered as I did then when the angel's proclamations would be revealed. Instead, all of their hopes had died with them. They died still wondering. Surely, there would be no harm if what the angels foretold us never came to pass. Only a few of us knew for certain what happened that night, anyway.

Who would have known enough to care—a few shepherds, a few magi, Simeon, and Anna? I guess that most of them had died since that night, now over two decades ago.

So would it really matter if God changed his plans? The magi were somewhere far to the east of here. Herod was dead. Nobody seemed to be thinking that their Savior was walking amongst them. For them, they were like their ancestors who waited for centuries for their Christ, their Messiah, to reveal himself. They, too, just kept waiting. I lost many hours of sleep trying to figure out what to make of all that I had experienced that night.

At times, I even found myself having doubts, wondering if it was all true and if that night's events really happened. Had we made it up? I could not conceive all of us, as shepherds, having the same dream. Maybe what others said about our having some mind-altering or spoiled food or drink was accurate, and we were just exaggerating. I did not, could not, and would not believe any of these doubts and questions. I was ashamed that these thoughts even surfaced, but too often they did. Decades of waiting is a long time.

Though parts caused me to question, one thing that I knew for certain was that my fellow shepherds and I believed we had visited the Holy Family that night in Bethlehem. That had happened, but could it be possible that we happened upon another young couple named Mary and Joseph, who could not find a room in which to stay and had settled into a stable for the night when their child was to be born? We knew the town was overcrowded. Others surely could not find a vacancy in an inn either.

No, surely not! What would be the odds? Further, I had seen the couple with their Son, Jesus, again in Jerusalem—this time a decade later. That meeting, those instances were real—not a dream, not some bad food or drink. Even Dismas had met that same family and held their son. Something monumental had happened. I was certain.

Regardless, I was ready for something to start happening. John and Jesus were now young men. Where were they? When would their identities and their missions be revealed? I was ready and anxious but also worried that it might not happen. I wanted so badly for it to be true. Clouds of confusion filled my head throughout these years, but whenever they surfaced, I convinced myself that it had happened and all was true. I found myself repeatedly, saying, "Maybe tomorrow. If not tomorrow, surely before next year."

However, another five years went by. I was now thirty-five, and Jesus would be twenty-five. Hannah and I, with our five children, were happy and healthy. My mother had moved in with us a year or two after my father's death. My brother and sister were now grown and had started their own homes and families. We were blessed that they both lived and worked in Bethlehem, just down the road. We got to see, visit, and care for each other often. They came to visit us more than we went to visit them since Mother lived with us. It was just easier that way. In the past five years, we might have gotten two letters from Dismas, which mainly said he missed us and hoped we were doing well. He said he was doing fine but told us little else. Without knowing where to send our responses, we could not even tell him how we were. He told us little to nothing about his life. We could tell him nothing about ours.

Still no word about Jesus. None from John either. The days of my thinking every day about Jesus were getting less and less. Over the years, I had told my Jesus story to so many. I am sure that, by now, most had forgotten. If any did remember, I was sure that they were convinced more than ever that my ramblings were just those of a young boy making things up. I found myself sometimes going weeks or months without thinking about Jesus. My life was complete. Not hearing of Jesus kept him in the background of my life. I was not happy with this development, but that was the way it was. I just went on with my life.

Everyday Life—Full of Questions

B Y THE TIME I turned forty, Jesus would have been thirty. I was now considered by many to be an old man, though I did not feel old. Men, in my day, routinely lived into their forties or early fifties. If a male could make it past puberty and not get badly injured, reaching a ripe old age of fifty or sixty was not out of the question. At forty, I still felt vibrant and strong. I could still lift huge and heavy stones for my building projects. My work kept me robust. My mind was still sharp, and I felt that I was still learning every day.

However, after the passing of three decades, I really began to wonder about Jesus and if he was, indeed, out there as my Christ and Savior. If so, surely by the time Jesus reached thirty, would we not have heard or seen something? At thirty, Jesus would now be considered past middle age. I could not figure it out. I had spent thirty years waiting for that baby to grow into manhood and assume his role as our King. For the first twenty years, I anxiously waited for Jesus to proclaim his calling. When he did not, I rationalized that Jesus was still young and maybe needed more maturity, more seasoning, more aging, and more sageness before the people would believe him. However, for most of the last ten years, I found myself more anxiously waiting and thinking, "Well, maybe today will be the day." Then I would find myself saying the same thing the next day.

I guess it is natural I moved on to other things more present and tangible in my life. Children, a wife, a mother, a home, a job, being a citizen of Bethlehem, and staying in Rome's favor consumed my attention. In my thirties, I found myself not thinking about Jesus for long periods. But now that I was in my forties, I found myself often pleading, "Please, God! Please explain it to me! I do not understand."

Living with family and friends to whom I had told Jesus's story became increasingly more trying. Every so often, these friends and family would bring up my Jesus story and say things like, "So where is this Jesus? Where is our Savior? We sure are getting tired of waiting. Were you not going to be in his army, help him overthrow the Romans, and usher in his new kingdom? You are now up in years, nearly an old man. You will not be much help to him now, especially with your family's needs. It has been three decades since he was born. We have seen nothing happen. What do you say, shepherd boy?" Most would just snicker. Some would laugh. Increasingly, I found myself only able to shrug my shoulders and shake my head. Walking away usually seemed to be the best course. Why? I did not have an answer for them. I wish I did, but I did not. I was more perplexed than they were. Hannah believed in me, and we talked about Jesus privately, but I quit bringing up any mention of him to anyone else. With no answers for them, it was not worth it.

Daniel had turned of age the year before and had taken after his father, grandfather, and uncle—joining me as a stonemason. In a few years, I looked forward to our other sons joining us as well. Some of my sons were starting, as I had, as shepherd boys. Some of the other children helped Hannah's father in his bakery. Hannah kept busy around the house, working our gardens and a small vineyard. She was an excellent mother to our five children. The oppressiveness of the Romans was as stifling as it had been my whole life. Bandits still tormented the soldiers and their friends with surprise attacks, robberies, fires, and mayhem. In many ways, nothing had changed since I was a boy.

A year or so ago, Judea was appointed a new prefect by the name of Pilate from the Pontius family. Pilate started badly, and time did not improve his performance. As prefect or governor, Pilate had significant military obligations. Shortly after his appointment, he became notorious for his famous "affair of Roman standards," as it came to be called. He had his troops march into Jerusalem displaying medallions and shields bearing the likeness of the emperor. As I mentioned to you and as I learned from my father, the Jewish people thought it an abomination and sin against God and our laws to have any object bearing an engraved image of a person. After a massive uprising by the Jewish people, Pilate finally relented and removed the depictions. His hatred of those he ruled started then and only grew more intense over time.

Soon after, Pilate got into trouble because of a project on which I worked. Pilate needed to improve the aqueduct system running from Bethlehem to Jerusalem. As I mentioned, my father and my forebearers had helped build and maintain the Holy City's water system for years and years. Pilate's actions addressed a major need for the city and its citizens. His decision would improve life; the project was needed—no one questioned that. A constant source of water is vital. The project's need was honorable. Where he went wrong was how he paid for those improvements. He took funds from the temple's treasury.

I have often wondered how he got those funds without involving the religious authorities. The temple's funds are stored in the innermost, most sacred components of the temple—in areas that Gentiles are forbidden to enter. People, like Pilate, are not permitted. Undoubtedly, the priests and their administration knew from the start what was happening and participated in the transfer of temple funds to meet Pilate's needs.

However, when the Jewish people learned that their temple taxes were being used for governmental needs, the nation revolted. Remember the Jewish citizens pay their tithe, the temple tax, and the governmental tax. Using the temple taxes for the government went too far. Unfortunately, this time, the revolt resulted in bloodshed. Despite these horrors, Pilate continued to cause unrest and brew hatred among those he ruled. It got so out of hand that Emperor Tiberius had to step in and ordered Pilate to uphold his Jewish citizenry's laws, practices, and religious customs. Over the next few years, Pilate seemed to be trying to do as Tiberius ordered, but it was difficult. Too much damage had already been done.

John the Baptist Finally!

The Voice of One Crying in the Wilderness, "Make
Ready the Way of the Lord; Make His Paths Straight."
John the Baptist appeared in the wilderness preaching
a baptism of repentance for the forgiveness of sins.
—Mark 1:3–4 (NASB)

E ARLY IN MY FORTY-FIRST year, when Jesus would have
been thirty-one, we received a letter from Dismas.
After wishing Mother and us his best, he recalled my
story of Mary visiting Elizabeth, her aunt, who in her old
age, was to have a son. He remembered Mary saying an
angel had told Elizabeth and her husband to name their
son John. The angel then foretold that John's mission was
to instruct the people on their need to change their ways
and become righteous and pure. They needed to hurry
and be prepared because the coming of the Christ was "at
hand"!

Dismas said that he had seen and met a man called John
doing just what Mary said would happen. John was better
known as the Baptist or the Baptizer because he was baptizing by immersing his believing followers in the Jordan River

as it flows through Judea. The Jordan then flows through Galilee and Samaria before it fills the Dead Sea, which is only a short distance east of Bethlehem. When baptized, the repentant believer's sins are symbolically washed away, and they are cleansed for a new righteous life. They are now ready to receive their Lord and Savior. John's favorite phrase was "The kingdom of heaven is at hand! Prepare ye the way of the Lord."

Dismas described John as a rough-looking, hairy-chested, long-haired man who wore camel skins secured with a wide leather belt. Despite his appearance, his voice was penetrating and mesmerizing. People were captivated by and drawn to his words. As John's sayings spread throughout the land, more and larger crowds came daily to hear his message. People were coming from all around, even from Jerusalem.

As John spoke, many remembered the words in Isaiah, which read, "The voice of one crying in the wilderness, make ready the way of the Lord, make his paths straight." These words from the old scriptures had many asking if John was a reborn Isaiah. Others were whispering that, no, he was the Christ—their long-awaited Savior. As I read Dismas's letter, I could feel his excitement and his wonder.

I decided then and there that I must leave soon to meet John for myself. I could likely make it to where John was baptizing, see him, and be back in a few days, surely no more than a week. After thirty years and all this time of waiting and hoping, it was hard to imagine the time might finally be here. I had to see for myself.

When the Baptist was not preaching and baptizing, Dismas said John would rest, eat, and talk to followers.

Dismas wrote that John's diet was strange because he ate mostly locusts, honey, nuts, and berries. During one of John's rest breaks, Dismas approached John, saying that he knew about him, his parents—Elizabeth and his father whose name he could not recall, and his birth.

"Zacharias—that was my father's name," John said, encouraging Dismas to join him and continue. Dismas wrote that he retold my story about Zacharias being unable to speak while John's mother, Elizabeth, was pregnant with him during her old age. He told John that God, through an angel, had struck his father dumb when his father doubted the angel's prophecy and instead said that he and Elizabeth were too old to bear children. Because of his doubts, Zacharias fell silent.

John laughed aloud, a most echoing, thunderous belly laugh, saying, "I would have loved to see my father speechless! As a boy, I have a hard time recalling him ever being quiet. God sure has interesting ways of teaching us lessons, true? My father, speechless? Yes, I have heard this story, but I still laugh imagining how he was bewildered, agitated, and humbled when struck dumb. It is hard to picture my Father not being his gregarious self. Can you imagine what everyone, and I mean everyone, in the village heard when he could once again talk after my dedication? I feel sure he told everyone to never ever doubt God and to learn from his lesson. He must have been a sight for all to see!"

When John heard that Dismas and I had met Mary and Joseph and our new Savior as a baby, John replied, "I await the day of his revelation. He is far mightier than I. I am not fit to remove or untie his sandals. God's kingdom is truly at hand. I pray you, too, Dismas, will repent of your sins and prepare yourself for our Savior's coming. You are troubled. Turmoil rules your life. I can sense it. Let me baptize you with water so that Jesus can baptize you with the Holy Spirit. Prepare yourself now for his coming. The baby you held has grown, and his time is near. You need to be ready. The time is at hand!"

Dismas wrote that he told John he felt his sins were too great. He told John that he was right in noticing the turmoil in him but that *hatred* was a better word. My brother told John of the Romans killing our two-year-old baby brother. From this atrocity, Dismas's hatred of Herod, the current rulers, and all of Rome had become so consuming that he was not sure he could repent or if he could change his ways.

Instead, he told John that he hoped to join Jesus's army. He shared how he longed for the day when Jesus would cast out the rulers, the military, and the Roman legions. Unfortunately, to do so will require violence for which he was ready. He could not see his hatred going away. Instead, every morning when he woke, he swore that today, he would do all he could to disrupt and overthrow the opposition. He needed to avenge Simon's murder. He had one purpose in life—to help return the Promised Land to its chosen people. If joining Jesus's army would make that happen, he would be among the first to enlist.

John instead told Dismas, with tender kindness, to search his heart, and seek peace, love, righteousness, and purity. He warned Dismas that Jesus's mission might be far, far different from the one Dismas imagined. He encouraged Dismas to repent and purify himself in the eyes of

God so that he could become the instrument that God and Jesus could use in the new kingdom. Dismas needed to prepare himself to be used for whatever role Jesus needed from him. He needed to be prepared. Dismas's only response was that he would ponder and pray about what John asked. I take it from the tone of the letter that Dismas did not accept John's offer of baptism.

Dismas's letter ended, saying that the number of people responding to John's message was growing and touching so many. Even tax collectors and some of the soldiers were confessing their sins and becoming followers. The numbers being baptized and becoming followers were so large that soon the Pharisees, Sadducees, and Roman soldiers began appearing on the riverbanks to watch and listen. Some of John's words were barbs focused directly on these religious and military leaders. John called them vipers and said that the ax was already laid at the root of the trees. Those who do not bear good fruit will be cut down and thrown into the fire.

John even went so far as to chastise Ruler Herod Antipas, saying, "It is not lawful for you to have your brother's wife." Herod had recently married his brother's wife, Herodias. John constantly condemned Herod for his wicked ways. Surely, these words made all who heard them think that a revolution was coming. Dismas knew that these incendiary words would be carried back and reported to Antipas and the religious leaders. They, with Rome's support, were always prompt to eliminate challenges to their powers. The authorities seemed satisfied with the status quo, but John was calling for change. This oil and water situation surely would not mix. John's safety was in danger. As I read, I wondered if this was part of God's plan that started thirty years ago? Was this the start for which I had been waiting so long?

Before I could arrange to go and see John for myself, word started trickling south from travelers and the merchants transporting their goods to markets. They shared that John's impact continued to grow throughout the land. Their stories prompted me to pick up the pace to free time from work, arrange for my family, and follow the Jordan River north to meet John.

When the next news came, I grew even more excited. Stories started spreading about one particular day. As John was finishing the baptisms of his new converts, he stopped and stared as a man waded into the river. There was something about this man that made everyone stop and gaze in silence. As the man entered the water, he asked John to baptize him. John's response caught everyone by surprise. John, looking the man in the eyes, said, "No. I, instead, need to be baptized by you." After a moment of each man beholding the other, the man then asked, "Please baptize me. This way, we fulfill all righteousness." With that request, John baptized him. As the man came out of the water, a dove came and lit on the man's shoulder. The heavens then opened, and a mighty, clear, penetrating voice said, "This is my beloved Son, in whom I am well pleased."

The people and John stood in stone silence, watching as the man turned his head to the heavens, closed his eyes, folded his hands, and prayed. Then as the dove flew from his shoulder, the man turned toward the opposite shore from which he had entered and left. Everyone watched him walk away until he faded into the distance. The only sound heard was the babbling waters of the Jordan.

As John turned back to face the people, everyone started asking, "Who was that?"

John said, "He is the chosen one. I have been sent before him. He must increase, and I must decrease. From now on, his light will brighten as mine dims. He is the one who will make the path straight. From now on, follow him! I have baptized you with water. He will baptize you with the Holy Spirit."

"But who is he?" shouted the crowd.

"His name is Jesus, God's Son, the Christ. Follow him!" was all John said as he came out of the waters and sought solitude to reflect and pray. Hearing the name Jesus from those passing through the region confirmed for me that God's plan was finally unfolding. Jesus and John—both unveiled during my days as a shepherd, revealed by my seeing where it began and by my hearing Mary's stories—were finally making the pieces of the puzzle come together. I hurried my plans to find where John and hopefully Jesus were together. Surely, I would find at least one of them.

JESUS!

And Jesus returned to Galilee in the power
of the Spirit; and news about Him spread
throughout all the surrounding district.
—Luke 4:14 (NASB)

F INISHING A FEW OF the jobs I was working on would
take another week or so to complete, but my trip
arrangements were coming together. A week or so
after learning of Jesus's baptism, some merchants came
through Bethlehem. They said the area north of Jerusalem
was abuzz with news about John and Jesus. Unfortunately,
some of the information was not good, while other parts
were baffling.

Dismas's worry was justified. John's barbs and the stir-
ring of the crowd's passions stung Herod Antipas and led
him to arrest John. Word came from some who worked in
Herod's government that, while Antipas recognized John as
a righteous and holy man, he feared his reach and influence
among the citizens. All viewed that Antipas had, indeed,
concluded that his authority and power would be best
served by keeping John in prison and out of the public's

eye. With the arrest, Antipas banked on John's followers dispersing, bringing the movement to a quick, nonviolent end.

Upon his arrest, John instructed his followers to follow Jesus, but Jesus was the baffling part. Since he had left the Jordan on the river's opposite shore, no one had heard from or seen him since. John had said to follow him; but no one knew where he was, where he went, or when he would return. With John in prison and Jesus's presence unknown, I canceled my plans to travel north and meet them. Hopefully, when Jesus reappeared and John was released, they would join. Then all would see the unfolding of God's plan.

As I have said, it seems that every time I think about Jesus, new questions start racing through my head. This time, I started wondering: What would become of John? Would he serve side by side with Jesus, or would Herod keep him forever detained? Was it possible that this short time of John's ministry was the full extent of what God had planned when God blessed Elizabeth and Zacharias with his birth? John's ministry seems so short if he is not released from jail. And once again, I asked, "Where was Jesus?" God had acknowledged Jesus with a dove and a loud voice, proclaiming him to be his Son. Yet Jesus's next act was to disappear. When would he return? Would he return, and if he did, when would he begin to rally people to follow him? He was to become the mighty counselor—how would that come to pass?

I had been expecting something to happen sooner than this. However, now that it had started, I was sure expecting

Jesus's revelation to be something far more significant than just being baptized alone in a river by his cousin. The dove and God's words from heaven were impressive, though I guess I was expecting a more earth-shattering revelation to more than a few dozen people standing by or in a river. Instead, I caught myself laughing and shaking my head. Once again, I remembered the one certainty that I came to realize many years ago. From the day that my Jesus adventure started, I knew that I could not figure out what God would do next or when. He always surprises me!

Over the next month or so, word started spreading about a man named Jesus from Nazareth appearing in Galilee in the town of Capernaum. As would prove to be true in the many stories that I heard about Jesus, his presence and words brought great joy and awe. His words of love and the hope of the kingdom brought happiness. However, his actions also brought stress and dismay. He constantly challenged society's norms and questioned the practices and principles accepted and promoted by the religious authorities. Jesus would not find or necessarily help make his pathway smooth.

The next wave of stories noted the abundant praise he was receiving from his teachings in the synagogues. He spoke with deep knowledge and authority. He spoke with passion, love, and promise. His words seemed to penetrate all who listened. His message resonated with the people hungry to hear God's word and those awaiting Christ's appearance. I found myself remembering Jesus, as a boy of twelve, amazing the temple leaders in Jerusalem with his insights and wisdom. That boy, now a man, was continuing his mastery of the scriptures and God's wishes for us.

One story made its way south. Jesus had returned to Nazareth, his hometown. As he entered its synagogue, he took the scroll and read from Isaiah, saying, "The Spirit of the Lord is upon me... He appointed me to preach the gospel...recover sight to the blind...set free those who are downtrodden...proclaim the favorable year of the Lord." Then, as he re-rolled the scroll, he looked at those in the synagogue, saying, "Today, this scripture has been fulfilled in your hearing."

I smiled, knowing that all Jesus was saying was true! Finally! His ministry and all that God had planned for him were finally here. I remember I must have said, "Finally," a thousand times over the ensuing week. I was so happy. However, the story went on to say that those in the synagogue began questioning, "Is this not Joseph's son? Is he not the carpenter?" Jesus, knowing their thoughts, answered, "No prophet is welcome in his hometown." After a few more verbal exchanges, the people became so enraged over Jesus's proclaiming himself to be the fulfillment of Isaiah's prophecies that they seized him. In their anger, they ushered him out of town to a nearby cliff, preparing to throw him to his death.

As the merchants told the story, they shook their heads, saying that the people there were unsure what happened next. Maybe it was the authority Jesus displayed. Perhaps it was the fact that Jesus had been raised in that village or that his half brothers and half sisters were present and watching. Maybe it was some unexplained miracle. Whatever the reason, instead of being thrown off the cliff, Jesus instead just turned and walked away. Others who heard this story said, "But can anything good come out of Nazareth?"

I began to realize the challenge that Jesus was going to have in making his people believe him. He was being viewed as a man seemingly no different from those to whom he was speaking, yet he was now also claiming to be holy, the fulfillment of ancient scripture. I began to understand how confusing this must be. Thank goodness I knew all of what Jesus was saying was true. Being a witness from day one let me see these new revelations differently from others. I, however, wondered what was next.

Every chance I got, I made it a point to seek out travelers and merchants coming from the north to learn what they knew about Jesus. Their stories did not disappoint. Word was spreading throughout the land of his many miracles. He was healing the sick. He even touched and healed lepers. Nobody could imagine even touching a leper, let alone hugging them. But that is what Jesus did. Many of these lepers had probably not felt another human's touch in years; but Jesus would touch them, love them, hug them, talk to them, make them feel worthy, and then heal them. With his simple touch or a single word, their skin cleared, their sores and afflictions gone. They were like new.

Jesus restored sight to the blind. He made the lame walk. People who had not seen since birth or had ever walked could instantly see or walk. Whatever a person's affliction, Jesus could heal it. Instantly, all were made whole! All were made well!

He cast out demons from the possessed. Many heard the demons say, as they left the body, "You are the Son of God!" People marveled that even the devil and his demons were aware of who Jesus was. In all my years of questioning, I never thought to wonder if Satan and his legions would recognize Jesus for whom he was. But they did! Even evil pronounced him as the Son of God! Unquestionably, if the devil believed, soon all people would believe too.

I heard stories of Jesus becoming friends with women, tax collectors, prostitutes, the Jew and the Gentile alike, the poor, the rich, the well, the infirmed, the old, and the young. He befriended those from near and far, whether of our culture or not. People were amazed at how children flocked to him and how Jesus made each child feel special. When children were around, pure joy, smiles, giggles, laughter, and comfort filled the air!

As I reflected on these stories, the words of the angels echoed in my head that Jesus was here for all people. I was beginning to understand those words better. His actions showed he cared for everybody, not just the Jewish people but truly all people. No matter their stage in life, their fortune or misfortune, their culture, their appearance, their age, their gender, their health, their similarities or differences, Jesus cared for them—he loved each and every one. He welcomed all. No one was left out. Everyone was special. Everybody. All people! Just like the angels said! But I must admit I still struggled if his welcome included our oppressors—Antipas, the Romans, our enemies. Could Jesus really include them in the angel's "all people" announcement? If so, I had a lot to learn.

Seeking Jesus

And He took the five loaves and the two fish, and
looking up to heaven, He blessed them, and broke
them, and kept giving them to the disciples to set before
the multitude. And they all ate and were satisfied.
—Luke 9:16–17 (NASB)

Jesus had a special group of followers he called disciples. Word spread that Jesus sent them throughout the land to spread his message. As the disciples interacted with the people, they, too, saw need and hurting. To ease suffering, they began performing miracles. As a result, the number of followers joining Jesus as believers was growing day by day.

Jesus often referred to himself as the good shepherd tending his lambs and his flock. Being a shepherd, I could relate. I had lived that life. Flocks depended on their shepherds for nourishment, protection, and caring—their very lives. Jesus was offering the same to those who followed him. I felt such joy knowing that lowly shepherds, like all people, were being invited to join his flock and follow him as the Good Shepherd. Finally, the merchants ended, saying they had no more to tell as they related their final story of Jesus getting into a boat, heading to a distant shore, saying, "I must preach the kingdom of God to the other cities also, for I was sent for this purpose."

I had to see him. It was one thing to hear others tell their Jesus stories, but I needed to witness some myself. I needed to see that baby now all grown and fulfilling the reason he was sent. While I was excited to hear of Jesus's message and miracles and their impact on the masses, I still did not understand how these actions would lead to the overthrow of our government. How were these stories going to create a kingdom? How would our Promised Land be restored to God's chosen people?

I could only imagine one possibility. Maybe Jesus's message of love and turning the people to God would unify the entire land for his cause. Perhaps then the government would see that it had lost its power to govern. Knowing that everyone was now unified behind Jesus, they would decide to give Judea and its surroundings back to their people. Maybe Jesus really could make change happen as the Prince of Peace. All done peacefully. Try as I might, I could not fathom any other way for Jesus's kingdom to come to be, but God had surprised me before.

One other significant change in the Jews' past had led to peace without warfare. It occurred as Moses led his people out of Egypt. Could the restoration of the land to its people this time be realized without weapons and bloodshed? Whatever was to happen, Jesus was building a massive following of supporters—his army of believers. Maybe Rome would see that it was outnumbered. Though

I wanted to believe this was possible, I could not see Rome giving up so easily.

Word trickled down that the religious scribes and Pharisees were increasingly concerned, asking, "Who is this man, Jesus? What authority does he have to speak as he does? Only God can forgive sins, not a simple man like Jesus. Not a Nazarene. Not a carpenter."

I heard that Jesus, knowing their thoughts, rebuked them by turning to a nearby paralyzed man, telling him to get up, take his mat, and walk. Every morning for years and years, friends and family had brought the poor man to the gates so he could beg for food and alms on which to live. He had not been able to walk since birth. However, upon hearing Jesus's command, he stood, bent over, gathered his mat, and walked away glorifying God.

Throughout the land, Jesus was healing those in need. Some were even being healed and receiving power just by touching his robe. Jesus healed whenever he saw the need, even if it was on the Sabbath. To the scribes and Pharisees, healing on the Sabbath was work, and working on the Sabbath was strictly forbidden by Jewish law. So Jesus questioned, "Is it lawful to do good on the Sabbath? Was the Sabbath made for man, or man for the Sabbath?"

To make matters worse for him, Jesus constantly called God his Father, making him equal to God. In the eyes of the religious leaders, this claim was the highest form of blasphemy. These pronouncements and Jesus's flagrant breaking of the Jewish law led the religious leaders to devise ways of dealing with him, even to the point of planning his death. Two movements began to develop simultaneously.

The populace longed to be in Jesus's presence. They hung on his every word and stood amazed at his miracles. On the other hand, many others were trying to figure out how best to silence him. They had silenced John. Was Jesus next? But if so, how does this fulfill what the angels told me? I painfully would later learn that the pending clash between the powerful few and the massive number of commoners would soon come to a head.

Wherever Jesus went, he drew large, stifling crowds—all pushing and shoving, trying to get close, touch him, have him heal them, or answer their questions. Regardless of Jesus's plea to remove himself so that he could pray, rest, and meditate, the crowds continued to follow. The excitement in all the land grew daily. I could no longer wait for him to come south, closer to Bethlehem. I had to go to him. I needed to find him wherever he was. Hannah agreed that I needed to go. She agreed to take care of the house, and my son assured me that he could run the business. "Hurry!" she said.

As I headed north, it was not hard to figure out where to go. Everyone I met had heard of Jesus. They would tell me where they last heard he had been, and I would adjust my journey in that direction. As I neared Galilee, I noticed that many travelers were not as joyous or as animated as the travelers who had passed by only a day or two before. Most walked by hanging their heads, shuffling their feet more than walking. I was struck speechless when they told me that Herod Antipas had beheaded John the Baptist.

The word spread that, while celebrating Antipas's birthday, Salome, the daughter of Herod's wife, danced seductively and nearly nude for Herod. Antipas was so pleased that he offered Salome "whatever she wished." After conferring with her mother, Salome asked Herod to serve her the head of John the Baptist on a platter. Herod was appalled knowing that John was a good and righteous man—even a prophet. But being a realist, he also realized that John could rally an uprising against him and his government. Herod no doubt remembered the Baptist's admonishment against his marrying his brother's wife. Surely, his wife and daughter wanted revenge, and John's head on a silver platter would show all the citizens that revenge was theirs. As a ruler, Herod must always convey that his word was true and would always be enforced. Despite his consternations and misgivings, he ordered Salome's wishes fulfilled. Word spread quickly throughout the land of John's death and of John's disciples coming forward to bury his body.

After John's burial, his disciples found Jesus and told him. When Jesus learned that his cousin—his friend and his forebearer—had died, he retreated alone in a boat seeking solitude and a quiet place to mourn. As he did, people continued to follow along the shore's edge. They would just wait for him to return. As they waited, I came upon them. It was a crowd like I had never seen except for the Passover gatherings at the temple in Jerusalem. There were thousands upon thousands of people crowded along the banks of the Sea of Galilee, near the village of Tabgha, just waiting for him to return. I felt sorry for Jesus that his popularity had removed his chance at privacy and solitude. As the hours passed, we waited, sat, made new friends, ate the little food we brought, and continued to wait. Over time, we became restless and hungry, wondering if Jesus would even come back to us. If I were him, I would just land on a far shore and slip quietly away.

Despite the uncertainty and the long hours, no one left, showing how much all of us wanted to see and hear him. As the daylight began to end, we saw Jesus coming ashore to much shouting and excitement. The excitement rose to a fever pitch. After landing and passing through the confining crowd, he walked inward toward a craggy, uncultivated area. The multitude followed. Once he reached a peak, he turned so that all could see him. His disciples came among us, asking us to sit.

How we were going to be able to hear was beyond my comprehension. We were so far away. As he raised his hands to let us know he was about to speak, the silence among the crowd of listeners was hard to fathom. Except for the occasional cry of a baby, a dog's bark, or a cricket's chirp, you could have heard an ant crawl. Though the land had an amphitheater shape, I knew there was no way I would be able to hear him from so far away.

Then Jesus began to speak in a calm, reassuring voice—just as if he and I were the only two in a room talking. Though I was quite a distance away and could barely see him, I could hear as if he were standing next to me. His words were so gentle, his tone so soft, and his message so touching. Looking around, all were mesmerized like me. We sat like stones unmoving but also like sponges soaking up every word that Jesus shared.

As Jesus finished preaching, he asked us to stay seated and be fed. Most of us just looked at each other, asking,

"Do you have any food?" Everyone was like me. No one had much, if any, food remaining after the long day of waiting. Some had been away from their homes for days as they came to listen to Jesus. As we sat, word spread that a young boy had offered Jesus his two fish and five barley loaves of bread. Jesus thanked the boy, took his food, blessed it, and asked the disciples to come amongst us to pass out the food. All of us wondered what other food was being offered other than the young boy's. It would take massive amounts to nourish the thousands of people sitting with me as only a very few of those nearby me had anything left to eat. Yet all were quite hungry. As the boy's meal started moving closer and closer, I noticed a few nearby families starting to pull out their remaining food to share with others. Their offerings were appreciated but so small and infrequent that they were not nearly enough to feed this vast multitude. Yet when the disciples finally made their way to the edge of the crowd where I was, they passed out as much smoked fish and bread as each of us could eat. The little boy's meal had become a feast for thousands.

As we ate, word spread that Jesus was walking amongst the crowds blessing them, giving them words of love and comfort, and healing many. For me, he was still so far away that I could not see his features. From what I could tell and from the crowd's murmurs, he appeared to be of medium height and thin. His clothing was a long oat-colored robe tied with a thin rope belt. I assume he wore sandals. His hair was dark and shoulder-length, and he had a relatively short beard. Word filtered back to us that he looked like almost every other man in the crowd. He had no outstanding features. He was like us, like any other citizen from the region. His calm, quiet, and gentle demeanor touched us all.

By the time the disciples got to us with the food, the other disciples were starting at the front, gathering the leftovers and struggling with the weight of their overflowing baskets. As we finished eating, I jumped to my feet and tried rushing through the crowd to see Jesus. Everyone else had the same idea. By the time I neared the front of the crowd, which had regathered along the shore, Jesus and his disciples had retreated to their boats and were off.

Though I missed seeing and talking to him, I found myself mesmerized by Jesus's message and in awe of the miracle of his feeding us. It was a wonderful, moving experience like none I have ever witnessed. It seemed that everyone there felt the same. Each of us had experienced something extraordinary. I am sure that the thousands did as I did and told every single one of their family and friends about the wonders of that day. Undoubtedly, the number of people learning of our times with Jesus would reach millions over time.

As I walked home over the next several days, I wondered if Mary had been there with Jesus and his disciples. What was she thinking of all that Jesus was doing? I wondered if Dismas and his fellow bandits ever stopped their mischief long enough to find and hear Jesus. Dismas had visited John. Maybe he had done the same with Jesus. I could only hope that Jesus would make a greater impact on him than had John. Perhaps Jesus's words would convince Dismas to be a follower, a convert, a believer. On the way home, Jesus's words echoed in my head. I was amazed at what he said and the blessings he gave. And to think I could hear him from so far away!

I remember that he taught us to pray, saying, "Our Father who art in heaven, hallowed be thy name, thy kingdom come, thy will be done, on earth as it is in heaven. Give us each day our daily bread, and forgive us our debts as we forgive our debtors. And lead us not into temptation. For thine is the kingdom, the power, and the glory forever, amen."

I was equally amazed at what Jesus did not say. During his message, he spoke parables giving us examples of what God's kingdom was like and how we were to live. However, never once did he speak of how or when actions to overthrow the government were to commence. He never encouraged the young men to assemble under the leadership of his followers, nor did he speak against those in charge or against their power. Instead, he more often rebuked the Pharisees, scribes, and religious leaders. He did not even oppose the government its right to tax its citizens. Word was spreading that he had told his listeners to give to Caesar what is Caesar's and to give God what is God's. He was more about loving God above all else and having us love our neighbors as we loved ourselves. This Jesus that I had held as a baby, this good news for all people, was exciting Judea. Beyond my comprehension was how its citizens were to overcome their daily struggles with the government, their taxes, and the never-ceasing oppression. He never spoke of a kingdom on earth or being a Prince of Peace. Once again, I had more questions than answers. I sure did not understand how I could be in his army.

On my long walk home, I was filled with the excitement of witnessing Jesus's speeches and being in his presence, even from afar. Yet I wondered how the words of the angels would come to fruition. Surely, their proclamation would result in more than the preaching of our need to repent and being righteous.

JESUS HEADS TO JERUSALEM

And He said to her, "Do not weep." And He came
up and touched the coffin; and the bearers came
to a halt. And He said, "Young man, I say to you,
arise!" And the dead man set up and began to
speak. And Jesus gave him back to his mother.
—Luke 7:13–15 (NASB)

WHEN I GOT BACK to Bethlehem, life returned
to normal. I continued to seek out the travelers passing through the villages and those who
worked in Jerusalem, hoping that they had news of Jesus
and his ministry. I often was not disappointed. I heard stories of Jesus calming a storm merely by waving his hand and
another of his walking on the water. Some told the stories
with wonder. Others told the same stories with skepticism.
Some believed, and some did not, saying, "Only God can
calm a storm."

However, as unbelievable stories began to merge with
known and trusted eyewitnesses telling these same remarkable and seemingly impossible wonders, the acceptance
increased. Many saw a long-term friend or the poor blind

beggar whom they had known for years now be able to see—all because of Jesus's touch. Many started to believe. Others saw their long-suffering lame relative now be able to walk all because Jesus spoke to them. These miracles led others to believe, even some of the most skeptical. If Jesus can heal these people who had suffered so long, then, yes, just maybe, he can calm a storm or smooth a troubled sea. Yes, just maybe, Jesus is the chosen one for whom generations have been waiting. Many, but not all, were beginning to believe that anything was possible with Jesus.

My excitement and awe grew when I heard a story from Nain, a small village between Nazareth and Bethlehem. Jesus was heading south and drawing closer to me. Maybe this time, I could see him up close. I prayed that I could talk to him and share my stories of being there at his birth. I so hoped he would remember meeting me after his family and I found him in Jerusalem. Would he remember his mother telling him about my visits to see him as a baby? I was so excited to remind him of my holding him, my joy of knowing his parents, and my witnessing his feeding of the thousands. I hoped to ask how his kingdom would come to be. I especially wanted to know when he would cast out the current rulers and their armies. Could Dismas and I join his army?

However, the Nain story that preceded Jesus was the most stunning any of us had heard yet. It had the whole region buzzing. Jesus had raised someone from the dead! The story spread of a widowed mother following the funeral procession of her son. Many family and friends from her hometown surrounded her. The large crowd demonstrated how much she and her son were loved. As Jesus and his entourage were passing, Jesus stopped to pay his respects and watch the procession. What he saw moved him with emotion. When the procession stopped at the gravesite, Jesus went to the mother, saying, "Do not weep." Jesus then went to the coffin, bowed his head, and said, "Young man, I say to you, arise!" To everyone's astonishment, after a moment, the dead man sat up, turned, and spoke. Jesus then said, "Mother, your son." This extraordinary event caused the word to spread throughout the land, even to me, saying, "God has visited his people!"

A few days later, though hard to imagine, the clamor over the raising of the young man from the dead subsided. That clamor was surpassed by an even more astonishing story. News reached us that Jesus had resurrected his dear friend Lazarus who had been dead and buried for four days. Jesus had been heading to Jerusalem when Lazarus's sisters, Mary and Martha, sent word from their home in Bethany pleading that Jesus come at once to heal their gravely ill brother.

Bethany is a small village like Bethlehem and close by. It is a half-morning walk northeast of Bethlehem as you head toward Jerusalem. I wish I had known Jesus was going there. Going to Bethany may have been my best chance to see and talk to him.

For years, it had been my hope that Jesus would return to his birthplace, my hometown, during his ministry. As he made his way south on his pilgrimage, I was sure he would attend many of the religious holidays in Jerusalem. However, Bethlehem was so close. I dreamed of him visiting the stable where he was born and explaining where God's plan had started. I would have loved to have him here, but I also had a selfish motive. If he had come, I could show all my friends and family, all those who doubted me those many decades, that I was telling the truth. It would be so wonderful to be able to say, "See, here he is—your Savior, our Christ—just like I said. Now do you believe?" That would have been such a glorious moment.

Back to Bethany. By the time Jesus arrived at their house, Lazarus had been dead and buried in his grave for four days. As Jesus approached the house, Martha rushed up to him, saying, "Lord, if you had been here, my brother would not have died."

Jesus answered her, saying, "Your brother shall rise again. I am the resurrection and the life."

Martha replied, "I have believed that you are the Christ, the Son of God, even he who comes into the world."

Mary, the other sister, then joined them, repeating, "Lord, if you had been here, my brother would not have died."

Jesus, seeing their sorrow, wept. He then asked, "Where have you laid him?" They led Jesus to the tomb but warned that Lazarus had been dead for many days and the stench would be pungent. Further, the decay would be advanced. Moreover, after three days, the soul would have already left the body. All that remained of Lazarus now was skin and bones. Undeterred, Jesus asked that the heavy stone blocking the grave's entrance be rolled away.

When the grave was open, Jesus turned his eyes toward heaven, saying, "Father, I thank Thee that Thou has heard me. I pray that these around me may believe that Thou didst send me." With that, Jesus leaned into the grave and, in a loud voice, cried out, calling, "Lazarus, come forth!" After a few moments, Lazarus appeared standing in the opening—still wrapped in his burial cloth. Jesus told the stunned crowd gathered around to unbind Lazarus and set him free. Later, Jesus and his followers joined Mary, Martha, and Lazarus for supper and celebration.

The news of Lazarus's resurrection spread like wildfire throughout the land. I am sure that everyone, from the poor to the rich, from the slaves to the leaders, heard that Jesus had brought to life a man who had been dead for four days. Jesus's words of "those who believe in me will never die" were on the tongues of many—being spread and repeated throughout the land. Little did I know, at the time, how irate Jesus's words and actions were to those in power. Now they also had Lazarus to worry about. Both, to them, must be dealt with.

Dismas's Arrest

Passover was getting close at hand, and I started preparing to go to Jerusalem. I would first make my sacrifice and then celebrate my Jewish heritage. I had already purchased my lamb from my relatives, who still herded the sheep and flocks I once watched and protected. It was far cheaper to buy your lamb and take it to the temple versus buying one from the merchants stationed there. Having the money changers convert our money at a premium into the required temple money was oppressive enough. However, then paying an inflated, exorbitant price for an animal worthy of sacrifice was too much. To me, this was religious-sanctioned robbery! So I always took my own animal.

However, my plans took an unexpected turn when a young man, whom I did not know, rushed to my house looking for me. Hannah told him where I was working. When he came close, I could see the panic in his face and demeanor. He said his name was Phillip, and he was an acquaintance of Dismas. Dismas had gotten word to him, asking him to rush to Bethlehem, find me, and let his family know that he and another of his friends, Gestas, had been captured by the Romans and thrown in jail. Dismas and his friend were to be charged with robbery, arson, vandalism, and other crimes against Rome. Phillip summarized by saying the Romans were accusing Dismas of being an insurrectionist. We both knew that Dismas's future was dim and likely short.

Phillip told me where they were holding Dismas in Jerusalem but was unsure if the guards would even let me see him if I tried to visit. The prison was outside Jerusalem's city walls near a hated place called Golgotha or, as the citizens called it, "the place of the skull." All of Judea knew that those held there rarely saw any mercy. Almost all were flogged with whips equipped with barbs or bone on the ends. With each lashing, the flesh would tear. Most floggings included thirty-nine lashes. Forty lashes were believed to cause death. Whipping someone thirty-nine times was as many as you could administer without actually killing them. As bad as that was, it was better than the alternative. Most prisoners, especially those held near Golgotha, were crucified.

Crucifixion was the evilest and most torturous punishment yet devised by man. The soldiers would strip the prisoner naked; take large, long metal nails; and then pierce the prisoner's wrists, nailing him to a large wooden crossbar. The crossbeam holding the prisoner would then be raised and fastened to an upright beam, which had been securely fastened into a hole. Once the crossbeam was attached, the soldiers would nail the ankles to the upright beam. As the prisoner hung by his wrists, the weight of his body would restrict his air passages, making each breath more and more difficult. To help catch his breath, the convict would push up on a small ledge the soldiers attached under his nailed feet. The ledge helped prolong the death, which was already slow and extremely painful in coming. Death could often take days. To make matters worse, insects, birds, and rodents would feast on a victim who could not defend himself. A worse death had not been devised.

A team of four soldiers typically executed each convict. While they waited for death to come, these guards' jobs were mainly to keep the grieving family from getting too close to the cross and stop those who overly taunted the prisoners. During lulls, the guards often played games and gambled to see who could keep the convict's clothes, sandals, belts, and other possessions.

Eventually, after massive amounts of blood loss and suffocation caused by restrictions to the air passages, death would come. The lack of food and water, exposure to the hot sun, the victim's despair, and the onlookers' taunts often sped death's arrival. If the soldiers got tired of waiting for the prisoner to die or needed to speed up the process, they would break the prisoner's legs with a mallet so he could no longer push up to catch his breath. Death then typically came quickly. After death, the soldiers would take the body to a nearby potter's field or garbage pit and toss it there to join the other smoldering, rotting waste and bodies.

This harsh treatment and the public's ability to view the executions brought about Rome's desired effect. All who saw this savagery knew the power and oppressiveness of their government. At times, crucified bodies hung on their poles lining the roadways leading into Jerusalem.

This punishment, which was handed out routinely and frequently by the Romans, left no doubt what authority was in charge. Fear was a standard part of everyone's daily life. Everyone worried that they or a loved one would be next. It did not take much to get on the wrong side of the Romans.

I knew there was little chance Dismas would be spared, but I knew I had to try. He was my brother. Though he had been out of my life for decades, I still remembered him as my big brother playing with Simon, laughing, helping Mother and Father, and working hard to better the family. He was, or at least had been, a good, God-fearing, loving man. Then hatred consumed him. Despite his change, I still loved him. I had no idea of the wrongs that Dismas had done over the years, but I was sure that he had done all he could to torment the Romans, trying to avenge, in his small way, their murder of Simon. I found myself grieving once again for the loss of little Simon. Now I was also suffering for Dismas—imagining what pain and suffering he would endure. Hopefully, some mercy could be found among the soldiers. I did not know how certain they were of Dismas and his crimes. Maybe what they knew would warrant receiving the thirty-nine lashes. Perhaps, with this being Passover, I could encourage them to show him some leniency. I prayed they would just let him go.

DISMAS'S AWFUL PLIGHT

I T WAS LATE IN the day on Tuesday when Phillip arrived. I was planning to go to Jerusalem anyway on Thursday for Passover on the Sabbath. With the news about Dismas, those plans changed. I hurriedly made my arrangements to leave the care of my family and business with my children and their families. I would go in the morning, Wednesday, for the half-day trip to Jerusalem. At the last minute, I decided to take Daniel with me, not knowing what Dismas and I might need in the coming days. Having Daniel with me gave me some flexibility. We questioned if we should take our donkey to carry Dismas home if he was severely beaten or, worse, dead. We finally decided to leave behind the donkey and the sacrificial lamb I had purchased so we would be freed to devote all of our attention to helping Dismas without the distractions of the animals. As religious as I was, my faith might have to take second place to helping my brother. Passover worship might not happen this year for me.

As Daniel and I hurried to Jerusalem, we found ourselves slowed by the ever-increasing crowd heading to Jerusalem for the holiday celebrations. As we pushed our way through, the words I overheard seemed to focus on the same three things. First, all were excited and were talking about the upcoming Passover celebration. Secondly, the news of Jesus raising Lazarus from the dead was on everyone's lips.

The newest topic, which I had not heard before, had everyone talking. Word was of the prophet Jesus, the Galilean, riding this past Sunday into Jerusalem on the back of a donkey. Jesus was surely coming to Jerusalem for Passover like the thousands of us. The disciples and his close friends escorted him. Word spread that Lazarus and his sisters were among them. While all wanted to see Jesus, the opportunity to see a walking, smiling, formerly dead man was almost as compelling. Regardless, the crowd was large and joyous. I wondered if Mary and Joseph were with him.

As Jesus made his way into the city, throngs of people waved palm branches and shouted, "Hosanna," as he rode by. The Son of Man had come to the Holy City. Others sang and danced. Joy was everywhere, though some commented that amidst all of this gaiety, Jesus seemed somber and pensive. While he smiled and nodded his acknowledgment and appreciation of those celebrating his arrival, he did not seem joyous. They were not sure why.

Under normal circumstances knowing Jesus was in town, I would try to find him and his family to renew old acquaintances. That would be a challenge with the thousands, upon tens of thousands, of people in the city, but it would have been worth a try. Maybe he would spend most of his time on the temple steps where we found him with the rabbis those twenty-something years ago. Regardless, searching for him now would be impossible as I must do all that I could to see and help Dismas. I knew my chances were not good on either front.

After a trip that usually would take half a morning, we finally got to Jerusalem after a full half day. The air was stifling from the heavy crowds. Having worked for decades on the aqueducts, walls, arches, and infrastructure of Jerusalem with my father and later with my son, I, along with Daniel, was familiar with the city's layout. We knew Golgotha was outside the city walls in the upper northwestern part of the city. I knew the area well because nearby was one of the several aqueducts which supplied water to the city. That aqueduct filled the Tower's Pool which sat outside the wall below Herod Palace and its three towers—Hippicus, Phasael, and Marlamne. That pool, used by many to gather water, was near the Gennath Gate—a main portal for entering and leaving the city.

Rome's ability to demonstrate its strength and power was well served by Golgotha, for that hill was often filled with poor souls being crucified for all manner of offenses, ranging from murder to being considered undesirable or a menace. Rome made it relatively easy to charge anyone with insurrection. Everyone passing by or getting water there could easily see the horrors they would suffer if found to be on the government's wrong side. Three poor souls were dying on their crosses as I came near. Even from my great distance, I could hear their screams and the wailings of their families. I guessed the hill would be filled all week with crucifixions. The scene was compelling and memorable. I am sure all who saw and entered for Passover would remember to be on their best behavior to avoid what had befallen those poor souls.

The terrain was rocky, with many caves. The land outside the city walls was used for cemeteries, campsites for visitors, olive groves, and vineyards. It also, unfortunately, served as the main garbage dumping site for the city's waste.

Near the Gennath Gate, I found the prison holding Dismas. I asked Daniel to stay outside with our few possessions while I tried to see my brother. After pleading with the guard stationed at the entrance and slipping him a bribe, the guard checked me for weapons and let me enter. As he told me where to find Dismas, he warned me to stay a body's length away from him.

The prison was dark, foul, damp, and moldy. Mice scampered in the shadows as I looked for Dismas. It was hard to focus; the stench of urine and feces was overpowering. That smell, along with the sounds of prisoners wailing from pain and hunger, made it hard to concentrate. Those not moaning were shouting profanities against the guards and those in authority. Most knew their hours or days were numbered. My imagination had not prepared me for the environment in which I found Dismas. It was far worse, far more inhumane, far more putrid than even nightmares would envision. It was awful.

After my eyes adjusted to the darkness and I had gathered my senses, I found my brother shackled and chained to the stonewall in a small enclave that kept him from the other prisoners. The chains restricted his movements to roughly one-body length. Around Dismas was only a tiny bowl for food and a cup for water. The room did not contain any trenches to drain urine or contain other waste. In that midst, Dismas was sitting there, hunched over with his head on his knees. When I called, he looked up. He was much different from the last time I had seen him. He was unkempt, and his face was swollen from the beatings he had received. His hair and beard were long, and his eyes dark. The whelps on his arms, legs, and backs were hideous wounds—many caked with dried blood. Insects swarmed, and rodents scampered throughout the scene. He attempted a smile, but it was evident that the effort was painful. After looking to see who was watching, I took the cup and brought it to Dismas's lips. The water slightly revived him.

After moments of quietness and my repeating several times, "Oh, Dismas, I am so sorry," Dismas shared his story. He said that he and his friend, Gestas, had met the notorious Barabbas a week or so earlier in Galilee. Barabbas was wanted for murder, and he knew that the Romans had every eye they could find looking for him. Descriptions and images of Barabbas were commonplace and posted throughout the region. Barabbas was massive in size. He wore a constant scowl on his face. The large scar across his left forehead, eye, and cheek was unforgettable. These traits—along with his soot-black, long, tangled, unruly hair—made him easily recognizable.

His crimes against Rome were severe. His mean spirit and disdain for and mistreatment of commoners caused fear throughout the land. If you were in his way, danger likely would find you. Though he was a local Jewish citizen, everyone wanted to see him captured. He was hated and feared by friends and foes alike. He was an enemy of all.

A shared hatred of the government and their Roman supporters was the thread that brought Dismas and the others to join Barabbas. As they plotted their next crime, all agreed that Passover was the best time to continue their revenge. They reasoned that it would be easier to hide among the hundreds of thousands of worshipers in the city. Plus, to keep order, the Romans would be abundant but divided into small clusters distributed throughout the temple and city. Thus, the soldiers would be easy to spot and avoid—or so they thought.

With that reasoning, Dismas and his bandit friends foolishly agreed to join Barabbas's gang. Monday afternoon, six of them, including Dismas, decided to rob the home and office of one of the temple's noted and leading money changers. A successful robbery would add to the crooks' limited resources while inflicting a significant loss on one of their enemy's most trusted and loyal supporters. Undoubtedly, the target and his employees had been making huge profits over the past four or five days charging exorbitant rates to the citizens who came for Passover.

All worshipers must pay their annual temple tax, and many needed to purchase animals for sacrifice. For either task, only temple money was accepted. This policy required that everyone change their Palestinian money into temple money. The conversion rate charged by the money changers was exorbitant. Barabbas thought that robbing those who robbed from the worshipers and the poor seemed like fitting revenge. Hoping that I would feel better about his actions, Dismas added that he and his comrades had been causing this type of mischief for years. However, they always used some of their take to help the poor, including orphans and widows. Money was a by-product. His goal was to hurt and disrupt the authorities and Rome as much as possible. The more chaos and the greater the pain—the better.

They planned to have one of their fellow bandits go to the side door of the money changer's home and office. That door was off the main street and secluded—not easily visible from the bustling street. They had watched the house and office for a few days. Every morning, the money changer and his employees would leave for the temple. Every afternoon, the wife would leave to go to the market, leaving a guard alone to protect the home. Then while the gang member asked the guard questions, two others would slip up from behind and club him senseless. Dismas winced but smiled as he said, "That will show that miserly money changer to hire only one guard to watch his office while he is at the temple swindling hard-earned money from the poor."

Initially, all went according to plan. They ransacked the house and office, taking everything of value, even to the point of stealing the clothes drying outside. Their efforts truly paid off when they found a horde of money behind a hidden door covered by a large wardrobe. As they prepared to leave, an older lady—they assumed the grandmother—arrived. She must have been living there but was unknown to them. They had not seen her in the days of casing the house.

She walked in on the robbery. As she screamed, Dismas and the others turned to look at her. That is when she recognized Barabbas and started yelling his name. Dismas assumed that the woman recognized Barabbas from his wanted pictures that were posted throughout the city. Hearing the name "Barabbas" caused everyone within the sound of her voice to start screaming his name. Before Dismas and the others could get away, three bands of Roman soldiers, coming from different directions, rushed in, trapped, and captured Barabbas, Dismas, and Gestas. The other three jumped the walls and were able to get away.

After being beaten, the three spent the night in prison. The next morning, Tuesday, they went before the tribunal. Before the hearing, Dismas was able to get word of his plight to some friends who found Phillip and had him rush to Bethlehem to find me and share the news. At the trial, which lasted only a few minutes, all three were found guilty of insurrection against Rome and sentenced to die. There was little to no defense allowed or offered.

As Dismas shared his story, he cried that crucifixion would have probably been his plight anyway if caught alone. However, being captured alongside Barabbas guaranteed that his punishment would be death. Since then, all three had been kept here waiting for their turn to visit Golgotha. Based on those already dying on the cross and the others in the jail sentenced before him, Dismas guessed that the day before the Sabbath, Friday, would be the day he would die.

As Dismas lamented his future, his anguish intensified as he cursed that his overwhelming hatred of the Romans had changed nothing. Rome's power and disregard for the Jewish people were as strong and disgusting now as when they had killed Simon. He wept as he said how sorry he was for abandoning our mother, our father, and all of his family. He cursed himself for not being at Father's funeral. He bemoaned not being there for us and for wasting his life. He had been ready to join Jesus's army but that had never come to pass. He cried about how much of a mess he had made of his life.

I did not know what to say to him in his sorrow. I, too, wished his hatred could have left him. It would have been so wonderful to have him as a happy, involved member of the family. I would have loved to see him have his own family. He had so much promise and could have done so much good. Instead, his anger just consumed him. I do not think I had felt such sadness since Father's death.

About that time, the guard came and told me to leave. As I left, I asked the guard the best way to appeal my brother's case. He laughed, saying that I could try, but my brother had a better chance of getting a bath, feasting on a sumptuous banquet, and drinking wine to his heart's content. As he turned, shaking his head, I asked if I could come to see Dismas tomorrow. The guard grumbled to come back tomorrow at the ninth hour, which was around midafternoon. If I brought the same incentive, he would let me in.

That evening, Daniel and I set up our tent upwind from Golgotha along with hundreds of others there for Passover. Daniel agreed to return to Bethlehem early the following day, prepare for Dismas's burial, and then return Friday with the donkey. It was impossible to know what the soldiers planned to do with Dismas's body. Often, prisoners were left hanging on their cross long enough to decompose and have the bones fall away and be carried off by the animals. This treatment was usually reserved for those criminals and their families on whom the leaders wanted to inflict the most punishment. Dismas may fall in this category since he had been caught with Barabbas. These poor souls would have no burial or tomb. The authority's goal was to ensure that society would forget them and no one would ever remember they had ever lived. This extreme horror was a strong motivator for the citizens to obey and never think of rebellion.

However, I doubted this would be Dismas's fate. With Jerusalem filled for the Passover and with so many prisoners, leaving the criminals to rot on the crosses was not practical. Frequently, the bodies were thrown on the garbage heap, though at times, they were buried in a common pauper's tomb. For those buried there, the family could get the bones a year or so later. However, I had heard of a few instances in which the family could take the body once it was taken down from the cross. In those cases, bribes were usually involved, but at least the family got to give their loved one a proper burial. The Sabbath and Passover would start that Friday evening at dusk and extend until sunset the next day. Maybe the guards would have some compassion with the holiday starting. A bribe would not hurt.

Further, to avoid even more hatred from the Jewish population, the Romans, for most criminals, did honor the Jewish law requiring that the dead be buried on the date of their death. I knew that meant the soldiers would guarantee that Dismas died before the Sabbath started. This way ensured no work—such as burying a loved one—would be conducted on the holiest of days.

Persuading the soldiers to agree to let us take Dismas's body and getting him back to Bethlehem to bury him before the start of Sabbath was going to be a challenge. With Sabbath starting at sundown on the day of Dismas's crucifixion, I could not imagine we would be successful. Getting him buried in his hometown before dawn on Sabbath morning was probably the best we could do.

Thursday morning, Daniel left early for Bethlehem. I went to the temple and its Israel Court to pray. My prayers were mainly for Dismas. I prayed that he be shown mercy and that he be returned to us. After prayer, I converted my local money into temple money and paid my half-shekel temple tax. I used the money to pay double the typical costs for a lamb to be sacrificed to atone for my sins. I kept thinking how ironic it was that I was likely paying the same money changers that Dismas was robbing when he was captured.

Word was still swirling throughout the temple of an event from a few days ago that happened in the temple's Court of the Gentiles. The story told of the prophet Jesus coming to the temple. In a fit of rage, he started yelling at the money changers. He exclaimed that they had made his house, which is to be a house of prayer, into a robber's den. In his anger, he overturned the tables and took a whip at the merchants, money changers, and animals, casting them all from the temple. Some laughed as they recalled the chaotic scene. Others' anger was still boiling as they recounted the financial and material losses that Jesus had caused. Their livelihood, their animals of all sorts—goats, lambs, sheep, cattle, doves, and pigeons—were running loose throughout the courts or had flown away. Money and items once for sale were strewn all around. Chaos was rampant. All wondered what would ensue from Jesus's actions once the priests and the government became aware of who had caused all of this unrest. Surely such actions would not go unpunished. Justice would be served. Was this the same Jesus I was expecting to follow as my Savior? I ran into all manner of men named Jesus almost every day. Was this Jesus the baby of Mary and Joseph? If so, I was struck by the fact that Jesus may be caught and punished like my brother for actions taken against these corrupt temple money changers.

They ended their stories, with amazement, that this same Jesus returned the very next day to the temple and preached on the temple's steps. They marveled at Jesus's bravery to return to the same place in which he had caused such turmoil. Many expressed hopes for his safety. Others hoped he would be punished accordingly. I found myself distracted with new thoughts about Jesus and chastised myself for not focusing on Dismas. I spent the rest of the morning and midday talking to every religious or political authority I could find. Some sent me to their superiors. To all, I begged for mercy. By midafternoon, I had not found one sympathetic ear. Bribes were not even an enticement. Catching Dismas with Barabbas seemed to seal Dismas's fate. Everyone knew of Barabbas and the great turmoil, pain, suffering, destruction, and death he had caused. Dismas's guilt by association was all that seemed to matter as I made my case. A brush-off and request to leave them alone was the usual response to my pleas.

Dejectedly, I made it to the prison at the appointed hour, paid the guard, and went in to spend some final hours with Dismas. I told Dismas of my efforts to have his life spared. To Dismas's credit, he was resolved to his fate, knowing that he had broken laws that were punishable. He beat himself up, saying he should have never joined Barabbas earlier in the week: "Why, why did I join him? I knew the risks. I had been so careful all these years, and here I go joining with the most notorious criminal in the land. Everyone knows Barabbas. The governor Pontius Pilate, Caiaphas the high priest, Herod Antipas the Tetrarch, the soldiers, the scribes, the Pharisees—everybody, everybody knows Barabbas! Since everyone in the land knew of him and was looking for him, surely, his days were numbered. So why did I have to go and join him? Stupid! I am an idiot!"

As time went on, Dismas lamented that, after tomorrow, life in Judea would be better off without him. He had caused more consternation than joy, more harm than good, and more pain than healing. I tried, though unsuccessfully, to console him by saying that his actions were driven by love. Everything he did was because of his love for Simon. He understood but kept saying that surely there were other ways to have dealt with the wrongs his enemies had brought on his family and his baby brother. I pleaded with him to pray for forgiveness. He said he would try, but he could not imagine God forgiving him. His sins were too great.

After a long period of absolute quiet in Dismas's small enclave, he said how he wished he had listened to John the Baptizer. He wished he had responded positively to John's request to baptize him and be prepared to follow the Christ, the *one* about whom John prophesized. He questioned if that Christ and Savior is the very Jesus foretold to me by the angels. If so, then yes, he is at hand. Dismas remembered that John cautioned that Christ's message and mission might be different from what Dismas imagined. John had encouraged Dismas to wait and see how God's kingdom would unfold and then see how Jesus could use him. Though that kingdom had not yet been revealed, Dismas cried how his life and those of so many others could have been so much better if he had listened to and followed the Baptizer's plea. Dismas cried out in a loud voice, "Why did I not wait? Why did I not wait? I am such a fool!" Those words still echo in my mind.

I tried to distract him from thinking about tomorrow by telling him about Mother, his siblings, my family, and especially my great fortune in finding and marrying Hannah. After a while, I realized that, while Dismas wanted to hear about his family, there was nothing I could do to distract him or lift his spirits. Instead, my talking only reminded Dismas of what he had missed. So with that, Dismas just sat there in the dark, damp cave shackled and awaiting his fate. I could only sit there with him, offering words of love and comfort. I felt so inadequate. Those were some of the longest hours I had ever spent. Sitting there immersed in the most profound sorrow and not being able to help in any way caused a feeling of helplessness that I would not wish on anyone.

Though it was impossible to know from the prison what the day was doing outside, I guessed it was getting near sundown. After a while, the guard came. He carried a perfumed cloth over his nose and mouth to counter the stench. Through his muffled mouth, he told me I must leave soon. I pleaded to hug Dismas goodbye. In a moment of compassion that I did not expect, the guard told me to do it quickly and then come see him on the way out. As he turned and left, I hugged Dismas tightly. We cried. Through our sobs, we told of our love for each other. I finally tore myself away, looked him in the eyes, and told him to be strong. I ended by telling him I would be there early the next morning.

I do not remember much of the rest of that evening and night. I ate little and slept even less. I felt so all alone. I am sure I fell asleep off and on but felt like most of the night was in prayer—prayers for Dismas, prayers for my family whom I am sure were already grieving after hearing Daniel's news. I prayed for Daniel's safe return tomorrow. I even prayed for Gestas and Barabbas and their families. Tomorrow all would suffer the same pains that Dismas and I would suffer. I prayed for God to give me—us—strength.

I had never witnessed firsthand a crucifixion. I could only imagine the horrors I would see, the pain I would hear, the anguish I would see in the faces of loved ones, and the indifference I expected from the soldiers. I could not imagine a worse tomorrow. Over and over, I prayed,

"God, give me strength to endure. Give me the strength to be there for my brother. Help me be strong for him. Let him see love and support through me—in this hour of his greatest need. Please forgive Dismas—his love for one turned to hatred for others. Please forgive him. Dear God, I especially pray that you give Dismas strength. Let him know you are beside him. Give him peace. Show him comfort. Let him know you are in his midst. Let him see some goodness, some kindness tomorrow. Let him experience some hope. God, I pray you embrace and keep him." Before I knew it, the sun was breaking.

CRUCIFIXION DAY

And when they came to the place called the
Skull, there they crucified Him and the criminals,
one on the right and the other on the left.
—Luke 23:33 (NASB)

UPON WAKING AND EATING some fruit and bread I had brought with me, I rushed to the prison. I was unsure when Dismas's worst day would start, but with it being the day before Passover, I was sure the guards wanted to get the day over as soon as possible. So, by the day's second hour, shortly after dawn, I arrived unsure of what to do. The guard harshly told me that I could not enter to see Dismas one more time. Mostly, I just stood there waiting.

In a few moments, some other men and women, who I learned were family and friends of Barabbas and Gestas, joined me. To the north, I could see the three upright beams on the top of Golgotha now empty, awaiting their next victims. About that time, four soldiers emerged from the prison, leading one of their captives. I looked twice and recognized the face that I had seen on notices throughout the land. It was Barabbas. I expected Dismas and Gestas to follow, but only Barabbas and the guards emerged. Where were they taking him, and why were Gestas and Dismas not with him? Confused as to what was happening, I asked the guards. All they could say was that Pontius Pilate—the Roman governor, our proconsul—had ordered that Barabbas be brought immediately to him.

Why? They were not sure. They were just doing what the governor commanded. Four soldiers with spears whipped the heavily manacled Barabbas to move forward. The family members of Barabbas followed behind. I was left with Gestas's small group of loved ones. I alone was there for Dismas. An hour or so later, my dread started in earnest. Four guards emerged surrounding Dismas, with another four surrounding Gestas. Both prisoners had been recently scourged as new blood flowed from their backs, legs, and arms. As they exited, each prisoner was given a heavy wooden beam, their crossbeam, to carry to their death. As the entourage plodded along and then up the hill, the soldiers continued to flog them as they climbed the mount.

Upon reaching the top, all family members, friends, those who came to chastise the prisoners, or those who just came to watch the ghastly scene were ordered to stay back. In due time, we were told we could draw closer to the prisoners. Looking at the three beams, Dismas's soldiers led him to one on the far left while Gestas was taken to the beam on the far right. The upright in the middle was left unattended. I assumed that middle honor was reserved for Barabbas, who surely would be brought here soon.

I could only imagine the joy that Pilate and his guards were having flogging and humiliating the notorious leader of the bandits who would be crucified today. Pilate probably wanted to enjoy that moment himself. Surely, making a public example of Barabbas would serve as a warning to all citizens that no one should challenge Pilate or Rome. Barabbas would likely arrive soon. I was sure that he would be close to death already after his additional side trip to see Pilate.

With great efficiency, Dismas's four soldiers had Dismas lay his crossbeam on the ground. After ripping off his clothes and giving him some numbing vinegar to drink, they whipped Dismas as they forced him to lie down with his arms extended over the beam. Dismas's cries of fear were heartbreaking. One soldier held down Dismas's right arm and leg. Another held his left arm and leg. The third placed a strong, firm hand on each shoulder, pinning it against the beam. The fourth guard, known as the centurion or squadron leader, positioned a large nail, the length of your hand, in the small of Dismas's left wrist. Then with all of his might, he drove the nail through his arm into the wood. The scream from Dismas was bloodcurdling. I jerked my head away.

About that same time, another yell came from Gestas as his guards were repeating the treatment. As I turned away, I covered my ears and closed my eyes, trying, to no avail, to remove the horror from my head. Tears rushed and would not stop. And it had only just begun. In a moment, the process repeated itself as nails were driven through the right wrist. Though hard to imagine, this scream was even worse than the first. I guess the second impalement now magnified the pain of the first.

In short order, the soldiers grabbed the crossbeam with Dismas attached and, using ropes and ladders, mounted the beam into a slot on the upright shaft, causing Dismas to hang by the nails in his arms. I could not imagine the tearing of flesh and bone caused by Dismas's body weight pulling against those nails. The pain and shock caused Dismas to lose consciousness which I thought was a blessing. While the guards were on the ladder, they fastened a sign above Dismas's head reading, "Insurrectionist against Rome." When the guards returned to the ground, they took Dismas's legs, bent them, and placed a wooden bowl-shaped fulcrum below his feet. Once in place, the soldiers held the legs as the centurion placed another board and nail at his ankles. The centurion then pounded that nail through both ankles into the upright. That excruciating pain forced Dismas back to consciousness, coupled with more loud screaming.

I could not face it. Never have I witnessed, heard, or even imagined such horror. This cruelty was unfathomable. How could people do this to another living being? How could they be so heartless? How did these soldiers live with themselves? Their day-to-day job was to crucify men, primarily Jewish men. Did they view their work as just a job and sleep well at night? All of us were horrified by the moment. All were crying and wailing. Some fainted. No matter Dismas's crimes, or anyone else's, no one deserved such an execution. No punishment should be this awful.

I guess I numbed to what was happening because I forgot about poor Gestas. When I looked over at him, he was hanging just like Dismas. The sign over his head read the same. Crucifixions often lasted days. Almost all took hours upon hours. All we could do now was wait. After the soldiers gathered their tools and moved their ladders, they told us we could come closer. I moved closer to Dismas. I was still crying. He was in so much pain. With his feet nailed to the upright, he used the balls of his feet and toes to push up so he could catch a breath. I found myself praying that death would come soon to save him from so much pain. No one should have to die like this. Between Dismas's unconscious moments, he hung there moaning and pleading.

Gestas, on the other hand, was shouting profanities at the soldiers, all of Rome, the rich and powerful. For revenge, he would try to urinate on the guards whenever they came close. Mostly, the guards just stayed away, sat, ate, and drank. After a while, it became apparent they were drinking too much. For fun, they gambled, rolled dice, played games, laughed, and told stories. Their gaiety seemed extraordinarily cruel when compared with the extreme pain and agony they had caused. The day was beautiful, sunny, and almost cloudless. A breeze blew gently from the west. If we were not witnessing an execution, it would have been a wonderful day.

As the day's third hour approached, we heard a commotion coming from down the hill. As we turned, we saw Roman banners being carried, followed by a group of soldiers, a prisoner, and a small band of citizens. We could see many people lining the street who must have come from their homes and businesses just to see what had caused such a disturbance. I assumed the procession was bringing Barabbas to join Dismas and Gestas. Many watching were crying, which I found odd. Why cry for the hated Barabbas? After the procession passed, the crowd disbanded and went about their daily chores and routines.

From my viewpoint on top of the hill, I noticed that the prisoner could barely walk. When he fell to his hands and knees and began to crawl, a soldier grabbed his arm and pulled him to his feet. After this happened a few more times, I saw a soldier grab an innocent bystander and force him to carry the prisoner's crossbeam. When the entourage arrived, we were pushed back and told to wait. The bystander then lowered the beam at the foot of the middle upright and hurried away. He, like us, did not want to be there. I wish I could have run away with him.

From the little I could see, the prisoner looked close to death. From my distance and from looking at his profile, I could see he had been badly beaten. The wounds from his beatings were severe and deep. They were bleeding far more profusely than those Dismas and Gestas had received. His entire body seemed to be covered with bleeding whelps and torn flesh. He wore a crown of thorns that cut deeply into his scalp and forehead. Blood was running down his face. The poor soul had undoubtedly been made an example before Pilate. The extent of his wounds convinced me that the soldiers must have delighted in punishing him for his years of crime against Rome. They had enacted their revenge with the brutal flogging. I had no doubt this was Barabbas. It all made sense.

The guards told us to step even further back while they nailed Barabbas to the cross so he could join Dismas and Gestas. With the nailing, Barabbas cried out but not as loud as had his fellow criminals. He seemed strong and courageous. I expected that of Barabbas! As they mounted his crossbeam to the upright, they nailed the sign of his sin above him. In Hebrew, Latin, and Greek, it read, "This is the king of the Jews." I was confused. I expected a sign like Dismas's and Gestas's or one saying murderer, an enemy of Rome, or something similar. But "king of the Jews"? After a few moments, we were able to move closer to the crosses. I turned my attention solely to Dismas, who had regained consciousness. Though in great pain, he was able to say some words of encouragement to me as he hung there.

Around the day's fourth hour, a group of religious leaders came to Golgotha to witness the proceedings. In their rich robes and headgear, I was sure they were holy priests, scribes, and members of the Sanhedrin. As they stood pompously before Barabbas, they spit up to him and said, "He saved others. Let him save himself if this is the Christ of God, his Chosen One. He saved others. He cannot save himself." Others joined in, saying, "Come down from the cross if you are the Son of God!" Others said, "Let this Christ, the King of Israel, come down from the cross, so that we may see and believe." The guards joined in, saying, "If you are the King of Jews, save *yourself*."

Barabbas—king of the Jews? The Christ—God's Chosen One? What did this mean? The angels had said that Jesus was to be the Christ. Not Barabbas! And what did the sign mean? What was the meaning of this taunting? The tone of the religious authorities showed their great disdain for the prisoner. What had he done to generate such hate? All were calling him "King of the Jews" and then laughing.

I could not help myself. I left Dismas and moved closer to Barabbas's cross. I could not get as close as I wanted, with the religious leaders and family members crowding around the foot of the cross. Finally, I was able to position myself where I could see the prisoner's face. Though covered in blood and despite his crown of thorns pushed low on his brow covering his features, I was sure that I had never seen this man before. I was also confident he was not Barabbas. So who was he? I do not know how long I stood there puzzled. As the mocking continued, the prisoner said, "Father, forgive them, for they do not know what they are doing."

In my confusion, I started looking around for answers. Finally, in desperation, I turned to look at the prisoner's family and friends who had gathered near. That gathering was small. Only three or four women and one man were there. Of the women, all but one appeared to be roughly the same age. The other had her head covered, but her profile made me believe she was older. As I approached them, the woman with the hood looked up at the cross and then at me. Then I knew! Those eyes! It was Mary. Mary—Jesus's mother! Why was she here? King of the Jews? Could it be that Mary was witnessing her Son, Jesus—the Christ, my Christ—dying on the cross in front of us? I found myself turning back and forth, over and over again to look at the prisoner and then at Mary.

Why was he being crucified with two common rabble-rousers, common hoodlums, one of whom was my brother? And where was Barabbas, if this was Jesus? A few things, but not many, became more apparent. This was not Barabbas but Jesus. Pilate's sign was right: Jesus was the King of the Jews. Here was the Christ. But why was he here—for turning over some tables in the temple? How did this coincide with what the angels told me that night Jesus was born?

I approached softly and said quietly, "Mary, it is me, Aaron. I am so sorry. Is that Jesus, your Son?" Through tears and swollen red eyes, Mary nodded slowly. I then said, "I am so sorry. I am here with Dismas, my brother, who is on Jesus's right. He was arrested and charged with insurrection against Rome. I do not want to pry. Just know that I am here if there is anything I can do for you. Again, I am so sorry. I cannot believe this is happening."

After a moment, she looked at me with red eyes and smiled faintly—an expression I remembered so well from so long ago. She reached out to touch my arm, saying, "Aaron, my son. I, too, am so sorry for Dismas and you. You were there at the beginning, and we meet here again at the end. I am here for you if there is any comfort I can give. May God be with you and Dismas."

With that, I squeezed her hand and hung my head, crying. After a moment, I turned and returned to the foot of Dismas's cross. After a long moment of composing myself, I said, "Dismas, that is Jesus being crucified next to you. He is the baby I held in Bethlehem and you held in Egypt. There is his mother, Mary. She and her baby are the ones I told you I visited so many times in Bethlehem after Jesus was born. She is the one with the penetrating eyes I told you about, and you then witnessed in the west. You, too, held him as a baby. That man beside you is the boy I helped find in Jerusalem when Mary thought he was lost. That is him! That is Jesus!"

Dismas turned to look at Jesus sadly, saying, "I was to be in his army. Is he the one proclaimed by the Baptizer? Why is he here suffering like me?"

While Dismas moaned and yelled out in pain, Jesus was courageous and strong in his suffering. Gestas was constantly cursing and screaming in pain. His taunts never stopped. Everyone on the hill was subject to his wrath. Having heard the jests of the priests and soldiers, he turned to Jesus and started aiming his abuse at him, "Are you not the Christ? Save yourself and us!"

Dismas, witnessing this abuse, shouted to Gestas, "Friend, do you not even fear God, since you are under the same sentence of condemnation? And we, indeed, justly, for we are receiving what we deserve for our deeds. This man has done nothing wrong."

For a moment, Gestas turned quiet. In the silence that had surrounded the mount, Jesus turned to his right and nodded this appreciation to my brother. Dismas—through all of his pain but with all the respect, love, and understanding he could muster—said, "Jesus, remember me when you come in your kingdom!"

Then, looking at Dismas eye to eye, Jesus said, "Truly, I say to you, today you shall be with me in paradise."

As I heard Jesus speak to Dismas, I could only thank God that he answered my prayers from last night and this morning. God had shown Dismas that he was, indeed, beside him in the form of his Son. Dismas now knew, without a doubt, that God was in his midst. Dismas had been shown goodness and kindness. He had found hope when Jesus told him, "Today, you shall be with me in paradise." I know that a crucifixion site is not the site for joy, but those words made me smile. As I folded my hands in prayer and looked into Dismas's face, I saw that, through great pain, he was smiling. As he closed his eyes and slowly nodded his head in recognition of the gift he had just received, I saw tears of joy roll from his eyes. I cried again, but this time for joy and thanksgiving.

I prayed that Dismas now saw his life had meaning. He would live forever with Jesus in paradise. No more pain. No more revenge. No more anger. No more mourning over Simon. I naturally do not know what paradise is like, but I have always imagined that it was a place of wonder and awe—a place of great joy, a place of no suffering, only love and peace. Today, Dismas would know firsthand. I knew that tonight I could sleep in comfort and peace, knowing that Dismas would be with our Savior.

As I reflected and savored the moment, I felt a hand on my shoulder. I turned and saw Daniel, who had returned with the donkey from Jerusalem. The shock of the scene had overtaken him. His face was deadly pale. His body shook in reaction to the horror before him. I thought he was going to be sick from the sight. He whispered that all the preparations in Bethlehem had been completed. He asked if he could return to the burro, which he had tied to a tree near the base of Golgotha. I told him yes. Though he had never met Dismas but only heard about him through me, Daniel looked up and said, "Uncle, I am so sorry. I am praying for you." With that, he turned and hurried away.

After a while, I heard Jesus's weak voice as clearly as I heard it that late afternoon by the Sea of Galilee when he fed the thousands with the few loaves and fishes. First, he said to Mary, "Woman, behold your Son." Then Jesus said to the lone man with Mary, "Behold, your mother." Even in his pain and suffering, Jesus was thinking of others. He was ensuring that Mary would be taken care of and provided for after his passing.

After all of this horror was over, I knew that I must find Mary to console her. I needed to be there for her, but I also needed to be there for me. I had so many questions for her starting with "Why is our Savior dying on a cross?" I could not understand how today fulfilled what the angels had proclaimed so many decades ago. I tried to focus on Dismas, but I kept finding myself so confused trying to understand how this could happen to the announced Savior, the one for all people. How was this good news? There was nothing good about this. It was sad and filled with death. It was beyond awful. All of the answers to my many questions over the decades—the ones that I finally thought I understood—all went away watching the tragedy of Jesus hanging on a cross by my brother.

As the day approached the sixth hour or noon, the beautiful day started to turn dark. As it did, the wind began to howl and swirl. Debris was blowing everywhere. Sand was pelting everyone and stinging our eyes. Lightning followed, with the rain blowing so hard that it was hitting us horizontally. Within minutes, the day was as dark as the darkest, moonless night. Hail followed. The skies were so very angry. Everyone crouched low to the ground and covered themselves with anything they had that might protect them. Then the ground began to shake and quiver violently. Slits and tears rippled through the earth. Men and women screamed in great fear. The lightning frightened the horses, causing many to rear and throw their riders, even some priests, as they ran away. The storm raged on like this for at least three hours. Nature was mad.

Amid this upheaval, Jesus cried out, "My God, my God, why have you forsaken me?" Jesus's voice penetrated the rain's drumming, the thunder's roar, the lightning's cracks, the tearing of the earth, and the screams of those cowering nearby. His question rang clear, loud, and strong in my ears! When he finished, someone nearby yelled, "This man is calling for Elijah. Let us see whether Elijah will come to take him down." As they wondered, I instead looked to the sky and echoed Jesus's words, "Yes, God, why have you forsaken your Son? He was to be our Christ, my Savior. I was expecting him to be my Messiah. We were to call him Wonderful, Counselor, the Prince of Peace just like the angels foretold. Instead, all I see is a poor man being mocked and dying this most awful, horrific death. Why have you forsaken him? Why have you forsaken us? Why have you forsaken me?"

I cried for Dismas, I cried for Jesus, I cried for Mary, I cried for me. I cried for all we had lost. I cried for the Jewish people—they had waited for so long for their Savior, who was now dying a humiliating death as a common criminal. All was lost. Where was hope? I cried for all that had been expected but was now not to be. Yet through it all, the lightning depicted three lonely men, soaked to the skin, all moaning and crying in pain, slowly dying a gruesome death on three separate wooden crosses.

Nothing made sense. I found myself in the most incredible depth of depression I had ever known—far deeper than my despair of losing Father or witnessing Dismas dying. I now had no hope. All of the expectations that I so excitedly anticipated experiencing from that starry night were now gone. Why were we here? All seemed lost.

Days later, in reflection, I remembered the ancient psalm, which starts with "My God, my God, why hast thou forsaken me?" Those exact words were the same Jesus yelled in pain and despair. When I got back to Bethlehem, I went to the synagogue to reread that psalm. In it, David expresses his trust in God though it appears God has rejected, abandoned, and forgotten him. Yet David cries out for God's help and deliverance. And God listens and acts. David ends his psalm praising and worshipping God. David's hope has been restored. Through all his pain while on the cross, Dismas had received hope. Was it possible we, too, could still receive hope? Could we be like David and Dismas? Was hope still alive?

While he died on that lonely cross, I wondered if Jesus was experiencing the same abandonment, the same isolation that David had experienced. Had God abandoned Jesus? Had he turned his back on his only Son? Did Jesus even know where God was? Did he wonder if God still loved him, and would God deliver him as he had done with David? Jesus and I were both in a dark moment wondering.

After the storm finally ended, though midday, the sky stayed dark, as if we were witnessing an eclipse. The rain stopped, as did the wind, the thunder, and the lighting. The earth calmed. All was almost as before, except for the gray darkness which settled over the land. Nearing the sixth hour on the crosses, things turned eerily quiet. The prisoners were exhausted and close to death. Though you could still hear their moans and constant agony, they voiced more silent cries of pain. All of us, as witnesses, had shed our tears to the point there were no more. We stood there emotionally and mentally spent. Physical tiredness, hunger, and thirst also settled in. It had been a long time since daybreak. We joined the prisoners in the quiet.

Even the soldiers turned silent, as they, too, were caught up in the strangeness of the moment. I am sure they were puzzled at the severity and darkness of the recent storm. It was a storm like I had never witnessed before or since. I am sure that the soldiers had seen all forms of behavior from the convicts, their families, and friends during the daily executions. Nothing probably surprised them. However, I could only wonder if they had ever participated in a killing like this one? Today, one of those dying seemed to accept his punishment. That same one asked God to forgive them for crucifying him. Another prisoner asked to be welcomed into another's kingdom and was accepted that very day into paradise. Then a storm and earthquake engulfed the land. Darkness, in the middle of the day, remained. What could the guards possibly be thinking as they witnessed this most unusual event?

In the stillness, Jesus whispered, "I am thirsty." Without thinking, I turned and grabbed a nearby jar of sour wine.

Leaning on the jar was a sponge attached to a branch of hyssop. I realized then the guards might take offense and punish me for being so rash. As I looked at them, they flippantly waved their approval. Turning, I raised the soaked sponge to Jesus's mouth. After moistening his mouth with the wine, Jesus raised his head, saying, "Father, into thy hands I commit my Spirit." Then, after a long pause, Jesus said, "It is finished." With that, he breathed his last.

As the wind returned and the darkness persisted, the centurion—the one who had nailed Jesus to the cross—lowered his head. In a voice barely above a whisper, I heard him praise God, saying, "Surely, this man was the Son of God. Truly, this man was innocent." Many in the crowd started beating their breasts in distress. In their dismay, they turned and left.

Sometime during the darkness and the storm, the religious authorities had left. Had they witnessed Jesus asking his Father why he had been forsaken? Had they witnessed Jesus committing his spirit into his Father's hands? Had Jesus's courageous death changed their hate-filled hearts at all, or were they just relieved to think that this rabble-rouser was gone and their problems with him were no more?

Though immersed in the scene before me, I noticed two distinguished-looking men, dressed in religious attire, slowly walk to the foot of Jesus's cross. Their demeanor showed their great sorrow at what had become of Jesus. For the longest, they stood there quietly, with their hands folded in prayer. After finishing their prayer, they turned to Mary and whispered as Mary nodded, placing her hands over her heart, swaying.

HURRIED BURIALS

And after these things Joseph of Arimathea, being
a disciple of Jesus, but a secret one, for fear of
the Jews, asked Pilate that he might take away
the body of Jesus; and Pilate granted permission.
He came therefore, and took away His body.
—John 19:38 (NASB)

WITH FOCUSED DETERMINATION, THE soldiers told us to move away from the crosses as they went back to work. Each group of four soldiers gathered around their assigned crosses. One soldier in Dismas's group held a large mallet. Without warning, he swung with all his might breaking one of Dismas's legs. A second blow quickly followed, breaking Dismas's other leg. Dismas's cry of pain was as bloodcurdling as when he was first nailed to the cross. The horror of the scene felt fresh. Dismas's inability to support himself with his feet and legs made it far more difficult for him to breathe. Death would now come quickly.

As the mallet was passed to Jesus's guards, some of the onlookers yelled that Jesus was already dead. To confirm, one of Jesus's soldiers took his spear and thrust it into Jesus's chest. There was no response from Jesus—only blood and water flowed from the pierced wound. Seeing that Jesus was already dead, they did not break his legs. The mallet was then passed to Gestas's guards, who quickly administered the same punishment, breaking Gestas's legs.

Later, as I was studying the Messianic prophecies, I learned that Zacharias, centuries before, had foreseen that "They shall look on him whom they pierced" and that the psalms had foretold that "Not a bone of him shall be broken." I witnessed both of those prophecies coming to fruition. Every day, I remain amazed that every prophecy I have ever studied about my Christ has proven to be true in Jesus.

Jesus's band of soldiers began removing Jesus from the cross. First, they removed the sign and then the crossbeam from the upright. Once Jesus's body was on the ground, the nails in the wrists and the feet were pulled loose, to be used again for the next poor soul. As this was happening, I noticed the two distinguished men approaching the centurion, getting his attention by showing him a scrolled parchment. After reading the document, the centurion nodded approval and indicated that the men should stay there. He then walked to the guards to convey the scroll's message.

While waiting, the older of the two men waved to his assistants, who were attentive at the bottom of the hill. I assumed they were his slaves. With the signal, they advanced to the hilltop, bringing a donkey. After the soldiers loosened Jesus from the crossbeam, they stood and instructed the two men to come forward. They, in turn, waved for their assistants to come to take Jesus's body. After wrapping Jesus in linen, they laid him across the back of the donkey and headed down the hill. Mary and Jesus's friends stirred and began to follow.

I rushed to Mary and said, "Mary, I am so sorry. You and Jesus have been such a major part of my life. I cannot understand how today fulfills what I witnessed with you upon Jesus's birth in Bethlehem. I am so troubled by all that has happened today with my brother, your son, and Gestas. Go attend to Jesus, but may I seek you out soon so we can talk and remember?"

Mary—through swollen, red eyes that were still filled with love and understanding—said, "Aaron, after our grieving period, please come find me. I will be staying with John, one of Jesus's disciples. We most likely will be found with Jesus's other disciples in Jerusalem in a place called the Upper Room. Many who have followed Jesus will be leaving soon after Passover, but Jesus had a large Jerusalem following. Surely, someone can help you find us. How long we will be there, I do not know, but please come. I welcome you. We have many memories to share. I will pray for you as you bury Dismas. Today, though, we can rejoice, knowing that Dismas is in paradise with my son. I must go. God bless you." With that, she turned and left, being supported by the other women and the man who had stood by her side throughout.

In less than an hour after Jesus's body was carried away, Dismas died. His struggles to breathe were beyond comprehension. Witnessing his and Gestas's last minutes was horrendous. As the soldiers began taking them down, I turned to Dismas's centurion, asking, "Sir, that man is my brother. We are Jewish. May I take him home for burial, just as Jesus was taken? I ask that you let me bury him before sundown as per our religious laws and customs. My taking him will save you and your soldiers time in handling his body and burial. Is that agreeable with you, sir?"

The centurion looked at me with no compassion, waved his hand, and said, "For a denarius, you can have him. He is yours. Do with him as you want." As I handed him what amounted to a commoner's full day's wage, he muttered, "Good riddance." Despite his attitude, I thanked him, knowing that we had received a good fortune in being able to take Dismas and attend to his burial today. I hurriedly waved for Daniel to come and bring the donkey. Time was fleeting.

Sundown was only three or so hours away. If we did not waste a moment, we could get Dismas wrapped in a blanket, place him on the animal, hurry him back to walk it would take to get to Bethlehem, and bury him before sundown. With Passover starting in a few hours, I hoped the city streets and the roads would be quiet and clear. We should be able to travel much more quickly than when we came to Jerusalem only a few days ago—which now seemed like an eternity ago. Coming to Jerusalem, we were so hindered by the crowds of holiday worshippers. Hopefully, today would be different and more manageable. Getting Dismas buried on time would be close. We sure did not want to break our Jewish laws. Surely, if we did, we would be forgiven for having tried, with all our might, to do as our practices dictated.

We were right. The city and the roads were clear of travelers. The few we met on the road surely did not want to stop a man pulling a donkey with a dead body clearly draped over its back. We made good time. Daniel rushed on ahead to prepare the family for our arrival. When I got to the family's burial cave outside of Bethlehem, the family was there with their spices, ready to anoint Dismas's body. After prayers, a few words of memory, a few passages of scripture, and many tears, the ladies quickly went to work placing the spices and shrouding his body in linen.

After more prayers and remembrances, the other men and I placed my brother into the tomb. As we departed, we stacked stones sealing the entrance. As we finished, the sky turned dark, signaling that night and Passover had arrived. We had made it. We were still within the first part of the hour of Passover's beginning. We returned home to have the most somber Passover meal of my life. Though extremely sad over the physical loss of Dismas, I joyfully told my family of Dismas's plea that he be remembered in Jesus's kingdom. I beamed as I relayed that Jesus promised him that today, this very day, the two of them would be together in paradise. It was hard to comprehend; but today—right now, the same day of Dismas's and Jesus's deaths and while we were celebrating Passover—their souls were together experiencing paradise. That image gave me such comfort on an otherwise awful day.

The next few days were emotionally and mentally taxing. I was fatigued from the past few days' stresses. While grieving my loss of Dismas, I found myself equally distraught and perplexed by Jesus's crucifixion. I had no answers as to why our Prince of Peace should die such a nonpeaceful, humiliating death, no different from a typical villain. He had been born as a commoner in humble circumstances. I could never understand why God ordained for him to be born in a stable. But to die in an even more lowly manner was far more than I could comprehend. While I was sure that Jesus was today with God in heaven and paradise, I could not understand what it meant for God's chosen people who were still waiting for their Savior, their Messiah. For those who followed Jesus, had they been saved of anything?

If Jesus could have come down the cross and saved himself, all the people—even the scribes and priests—would have believed and rejoiced, proclaiming him to be their long-awaited Messiah. That did not happen. Instead, he died and was taken away on a donkey for burial, just as we did with Dismas. Our proclaimed Son of God now lay, decaying in a cold stone tomb, just like Dismas. He would likely be remembered only by Mary, his family, his closest friends and followers, and a shepherd boy from Bethlehem.

After a week of mourning, I told Hannah that I must return to Jerusalem to find Mary. While the Jewish grieving period was usually thirty days, I knew I had to find Mary and speak with her before she possibly left Jerusalem for areas unknown. I wanted desperately to comfort her, but I wanted equally to talk to her in hopes she could comfort me. I prayed that she could help me understand Jesus's mission. Why had he come to earth, why had God and his messengers proclaimed him for greatness, and why then let him be so cruelly crucified? What had gone wrong? I could not ask this of Mary, but I wondered—had Jesus disappointed or angered God? If so, whatever happened must have been recent. Only a few years ago, Jesus had been baptized by John. As John raised Jesus from the Jordan River, God descended in the form of a dove and said, "This is my beloved Son, in whom I am well pleased." God was happy with Jesus then. Had something happened in the past few years?

Hannah understood my urgency. She, too, did not understand Jesus's story but understood my need to go and find some answers. For over thirty years, Jesus had shaped my life. Almost every day, questions about his coming and mission and my role in them had filled my days. Hannah knew I would never find peace, never find rest, until I understood what it all meant. Surely, Jesus's life made sense. I just had to figure it out. Daniel readily agreed to watch the business, saying not to worry. He, too, would pray that I find answers.

I headed back to Jerusalem with some clothes, a few provisions, and a bedroll. I did not even take the donkey to carry a tent and the few other items that I knew I would need. I just did not want to be burdened with having to take care of those types of arrangements. Instead, I would sleep under the stars and buy food from farmers or vendors as needed. My career required me to interact with several of the contractors and merchants who lived in Jerusalem. Maybe one of them would let me stay with him and his family. I did not really care about my quarters over the next few days. I had one goal—to find Mary.

Trying to Find Mary

> But on the first day of the week, at early dawn,
> they came to the tomb, bringing the spices which
> they had prepared and they found the stone rolled
> away from the tomb, but when they entered,
> they did not find the body of the Lord Jesus.
> —Luke 24:1-2 (NASB)

As I walked to Jerusalem, I encountered more than one group of stragglers who were late in leaving Passover or were leaving Jerusalem for other reasons. Many were resting under the shade or along the sides of the road. Most were animated with excitement. Yet all seemed bewildered, confused and questioning. When I stopped for a break and joined them, I found myself lingering much longer than expected. Their conversations were consumed with strange stories of how Passover had ended and how the following week had begun.

Stories were flying that the Nazarene—the Carpenter, the Rabbi Jesus, the one crucified on Friday—was now missing from his grave. Word was spreading like wildfire that he had risen from the dead and was alive. Many recalled that

Jesus had raised Lazarus, Jairus's daughter, and the dead son at his own funeral. Though seemingly impossible, Jesus raising himself from the dead was not as improbable as it would have seemed only a few months ago.

Some questioned if Jesus was truly dead when he was taken down from the cross. Maybe he somehow survived and was now recuperating in someone's home. If so, how did he get there? After a few months, perhaps the plan was for Jesus to reappear healthy and well. Unquestionably, then, all the land would believe in him as their Christ and Savior, their Messiah. Most agreed pretty quickly that this was virtually impossible. Jesus had been sent to Golgotha directly from Pontius Pilate for crucifixion. There would be no way that the soldiers would ever let Jesus leave the cross without doubly ensuring that he was dead. Failure to do so would surely mean their own death. All concluded quickly that Jesus was dead when he left the Skull.

Some were saying that his disciples must have stolen his dead body to prove that he was the Son of God. The disappearance, along with great proclamations by the disciples, would help make willing believers want to continue following Jesus's message and believe. Others guessed that the priests and government took the body, but no one could come up with a good reason for their doing so. How would this help their goal of eliminating the blasphemy they felt was Jesus? No, this theory would not help the authorities convey they were rid of Jesus. Despite all of these conjectures, one thing was certain—after an entire week, no one knew where to find Jesus's body.

A few others said they heard that some women had been the first to see him alive and well, and it was these women who spread the word of Jesus's resurrection. This suggestion brought laughter as some said, "Women? You cannot trust the words of a woman!"

Word was even spreading that Roman guards had been stationed outside of Jesus's tomb to ensure the body was not stolen and made to disappear. The story rumored that the guards must have fallen asleep while watching the tomb and someone had come while they were asleep and stolen the body. That ridiculous notion brought even greater laughter than the story of women proclaiming that Jesus rose from the grave. Neglecting their soldierly duties was a sure way to guarantee that the guards would be severely punished—flogged at best, most likely meeting the same fate as Jesus on a cross. Can you imagine the guards telling Pontius Pilate that Jesus just disappeared and Pilate accepting that? No, it was impossible to imagine the guards not being at their highest attention, ensuring nothing happened to Jesus. Maybe one of the many soldiers had fallen asleep, but surely not all of them at the same time! And for all to be asleep while someone noisily rolled away a massive stone to open the tomb —impossible! No, the guard's very lives depended on staying awake and following orders. They had not fallen asleep. Yet the word was that Jesus was gone! Whatever the story, news of the disappearance could not be welcomed by either the religious leaders, the government, or Rome. Their rabble-rouser was still out there, causing trouble, whether dead or alive.

My contribution to the conversations was my confirmation that I knew, without a doubt, that Jesus had been crucified and had died. I told them about my being there all day witnessing my brother's death on the cross to Jesus's right. Many remembered when I told them about the story of Jesus calming the storm while boating in Galilee. I then described the violent storm and the darkness that enveloped the land while Jesus was dying. If God's Son could calm a storm in times of peace, surely God could send a dark, violent storm letting everyone know his anger at what people were doing to his Son.

As I reminded them of the storm and the darkness that encompassed the land, all became excited, finally understanding the reasoning for the midday, nightlike storm each had experienced. Next, I told them of Jesus's sayings while on the cross, including him telling my brother that they would be together in paradise that very day. I described Jesus's death and his being pierced by the spear. That piercing convinced the guards that he was dead. Further, the soldiers then did not break Jesus's legs, as they had done to the two other prisoners. Their not breaking Jesus's legs was proof enough the soldiers believed Jesus to be dead. Finally, I told them about Jesus being taken down from the cross and being taken away for burial by two religiously attired men. We all agreed that the soldiers would never let Jesus out of their sight unless they were confident of his death. Just like the guards at the tomb, the crucifixion soldiers would not fail their duties. To them, Jesus was dead!

On top of that, my own eyes told me Jesus was dead. I told the travelers that I watched as he was removed from the cross, as he was wrapped and placed on the donkey and carried away, followed by his loved ones. There was no life there—none! He was dead. I was certain. The soldiers were certain. As I headed on to Jerusalem, I was confident the travelers no longer questioned Jesus's death. What happened to him afterward was still unclear. I was now as confused as ever—maybe more. This new information only intensified my urgency in finding and talking with Mary.

With each encounter with travelers leaving Jerusalem, I asked if anyone knew of a place in the Holy City called the Upper Room. None knew of its whereabouts. When I asked if any knew or had seen any of Jesus's disciples or his key followers, some said they knew a disciple or two but that they thought they had gone into hiding following Jesus's crucifixion. It was as if all of Jesus's friends and followers had disappeared. Naturally, they were worried that Jesus's fate awaited them if they were found to be linked to Jesus, the blasphemer. Most of the travelers said that, if it were them, they would now be as far away from Jerusalem as possible. They wished me luck in finding any of them— all saying I was going to need it.

They were right. Finding Mary was more challenging than I expected. When I would ask someone if they could help me find any of Jesus's followers, most would just become quiet and turn away without saying a word. Some accused me of being a spy for the priests or Pilate. By now, most of the citizens believed that wiping out the Jesus movement was the religious and political leaders' goal. To be successful, those following Jesus must be found and silenced by whatever method was needed.

Though quietly mumbled, it was easy to sense the hatred that many carried for Pilate's killing of an innocent man. They condemned Pilate's cowardice in holding Jesus's many trials and final sentence in the early morning hours before most of the citizens were even awake to protest. Their hate spilled over against the temple leaders for their part in Jesus's killing. In their eyes, Pilate, the Romans, and the religious leaders—all those in any form of power—were equally guilty.

The Upper Room

When therefore it was evening, on that day, the first day
of the week, and when the doors were shut where the
disciples were, for fear of the Jews, Jesus came and stood
in their midst, and said to them, "Peace be with you."
—John 20:19 (NASB)

AFTER HOURS OF DEDUCTION, directional fin-
ger-pointing, and the process of elimination, I
knocked on a door asking if Mary was there. If
so, would they tell her Aaron would like to see her? The
person behind the door's portal told me to wait and closed
the portal. After a long moment, the door cracked, and the
eyes that I had seen before stared back at me. In a second,
they brightened, and the door swung open wide. There
standing before me was Mary!

I did not know what I was expecting to find. Her son
had been crucified a week ago. If the body had been stolen, her grief would be even greater, with her not knowing where he was. If Jesus had somehow survived and was
recovering, she would be relieved but worried. If Jesus had
been raised from the dead, Mary would be full of joy. The

Mary I found was full of joy! She grabbed my arm, pulling me into a room filled with people. After quickly locking the door behind me, she excitedly introduced me, sharing our brief history. She quickly told me the names of the few dozen men and women gathered there, adding that they were Jesus's disciples and followers. These were Jesus's closest apostles.

Though I cannot remember them all, I remember a few of their names. Present was Peter, James, John, Andrew, Mary of Magdalene, another Mary, Joanna, and Bartholomew. After they heard Mary's story, they jumped up, embraced me, and called me, "Brother!" After we joined them in some food and drink, Mary excused us, saying she had so much to tell me and that we would be in the adjoining room.

Mary's eyes danced with excitement. "Aaron, you will not believe what has happened! Jesus has risen from the dead! I have seen him twice! He is alive! Though I saw him dead at Golgotha, saw him anointed for burial, and saw him placed in a borrowed tomb, Jesus appeared in this very room last Sunday—the Sunday after his Friday crucifixion. Aaron, though the door was locked as it was when you arrived, we found Jesus standing in our presence. Naturally, we were startled and frightened, thinking we were seeing a spirit.

But then in the calm, reassuring words we have come to know of Jesus, he said, "Peace be with you." His smile comforted us as he said, "Why are you troubled, and why do doubts arise in your hearts? See my hands and my feet that it is I myself. Touch me and see, for a spirit does not have flesh and bones as you see that I have."

Mary continued, "Though we were having a hard time believing what we were seeing with our very own eyes, we touched his hands. We saw his pierced feet and the ugly wound in his side made by the spear. Even the scars on his forehead from that awful crown of thorns remained.

"It was probably just a moment, but it seemed like forever that we just stood there, looking into Jesus's eyes, not really knowing what to do. Thank goodness for Peter, who finally broke the silence, saying, 'My Lord!' With that, we all started hugging Jesus and each other. We were literally jumping for joy. Mary Magdalene and Joanna were yelling, 'See! We told you! We told you we saw Jesus this morning!' I wish I could describe it better. Maybe you can see it in my face."

I beamed, "Mary, I see it. Your whole body is filled with excitement. I see it in your eyes. They are the happiest eyes I have ever seen." Mary was so excited to tell me everything.

She continued, "Then, Aaron, guess what Jesus did next."

"Mary, everything you have told me is so unreal. I can only guess, but have no idea."

With a smile so wide, Mary said, "Aaron, Jesus asked if we had anything to eat. Can you believe it? He was hungry! We, then, feasted on broiled fish, bread, vegetables, and fruit. Aaron, I could not quit thinking that spirits do not eat. Only flesh and blood eat and drink. My Son, Jesus, is alive. He dined with us—just like before—well, in some sense like before. Here my Son was—once alive, then dead, and now alive again. I still cannot believe it!

"During the meal, Jesus obviously knew we were questioning everything—his life, his death, his resurrection, and even him. Who was he really? To help us understand, he said, 'These are my words which I spoke to you while I was still with you, that all things which are written about me in the law of Moses and the prophets, and the psalms must be fulfilled. Thus, it is written that the Christ should suffer and rise again from the dead on the third day and that repentance for the forgiveness of sins should be proclaimed in his name to all the nations, beginning from Jerusalem. You are witnesses of these things.'"

As he made this announcement, it was as if our minds started to open and our thinking clearer. The scriptures and his message, his purpose in coming, and his paving the way for those who believe that they can now share his kingdom started to come together in our understanding. Jesus sacrificed himself to forgive us for our sins. God gave up his Son for us. Just like those of our faith who sacrifice an unblemished lamb, like you used to raise to atone for the donor's sins, Jesus became our lamb who took our sins upon his shoulders and died for us. He is our sacrificial lamb—sacrificed for you and me and all who believe!

"Then, Aaron, he left just as he had come. One moment he was there, and the next, he was gone. When we finally started talking again, we found that all of us were thinking the same thing. We had been in the presence of holiness. If there had ever been any doubt, we now know with certainty that Jesus was truly our Savior and our God.

He was the Messiah for whom we had been waiting. In the days following, Aaron, I thought of you often. All the announcements of the angels that very first night had come true. The words you heard pronouncing that good news had come for everyone were true! You heard them say and sing it. Aaron, we are so blessed! I am so happy." And with that, Mary cried tears of joy.

"Mary, you said that you have seen the risen Jesus twice. What happened the second time?"

Mary smiled, saying, "When Jesus arrived the first time, ten of his twelve disciples were with us. One of the disciples, Judas Iscariot, had betrayed Jesus. He turned Jesus over to the soldiers and priests. That betrayal put everything in motion that led to Jesus's crucifixion. We learned that the morning after his betrayal, Judas committed suicide by hanging himself. We can only guess that Judas expected a different outcome for Jesus than he saw unfolding. Not being able to bear what he saw happening, his grief may have led him to kill himself. We will never honestly know what Judas was thinking or why he did what he did, but his actions led to Jesus's death.

"The other missing disciple that first time was Thomas, who was away on an errand. When he returned, we yelled, 'We have seen the Lord! He has arisen!' Even though all of us vouched for Jesus's resurrection, Thomas remained doubtful, saying, 'Unless I see in his hands the imprint of the nails and put my finger into the place of the nails and put my hand into his side, I will not believe.' Yesterday, just like that first time, Jesus appeared from nowhere in our locked room, but this time, all eleven disciples were present—Thomas included.

Jesus once again said, 'Peace be with you.' Jesus then immediately turned to Thomas and said, 'Reach here your finger, and see my hands, and reach here your hand and put it into my side, and be not unbelieving but believing.' As Thomas did as Jesus instructed, he dropped to his knees, saying, 'My Lord and my God!' Jesus answered, 'Because you have seen me, have you believed? Blessed are they who did not see and yet believed.' Thomas, still on his knees with his head bowed, said, 'Father, forgive my doubts. I believe. You are my risen Lord and my God!'"

"Mary, this is beyond wonderful that Jesus is alive. I can understand Judas's betrayal led to Jesus being arrested, but on what grounds was he charged that would warrant such an awful death?"

Mary told me that five or six days before Passover, Jesus had entered the city riding a donkey and began teaching and healing. The next day, he entered the temple and became enraged by the commerce being conducted on the temple's grounds. I interrupted Mary, telling her that I had heard about these events.

She continued telling about the large number of animals being offered there for sacrifice—all being sold at exorbitant prices by the merchants and greedy money changers. Their presence led Jesus to grab a whip, turn over the tables, and shout, "My house shall be called a house of prayer for all the nations, but you are making it a robber's den!"

"Aaron, Jesus cleared the temple. But only for a moment. After Jesus calmed and left, they returned, setting up shop once again. But, Aaron, I think that was the proverbial 'straw that broke the camel's back.' As you know, Pilate and Herod Antipas only live in Jerusalem during Jewish festivals and special occasions. I think that Jesus's cleansing of the temple fueled the chief priests' desires to kill Jesus and restore Jerusalem to their own beliefs and control. As you know, during most of the year, the religious authorities have the real power in Jerusalem. Pilate is only here during the festivals. Judas's offer to betray Jesus was the opportunity the rulers needed. Judas was always money-hungry. I wonder how much he was paid to betray my son.

"I understand that during Jesus's trial, he was charged with blasphemy, rebellion, and treason. Jesus's saying that he was the Son of God was so blasphemous in their eyes that I heard Caiaphas, the high priest, tore his robes in anguish upon hearing these words. The religious authorities then stressed to Pontius Pilate that Jesus proclaimed to be a King. Proclaiming to be a King was treasonous before Caesar and Rome. The priests stressed that Jesus's self-proclaimed kingdom could not rule while Caesar and Rome were in charge.

"Word has reached us that the religious authorities even threatened Pilate, saying that if he did not squelch this threat, they would report his failure to Rome. If Rome were to hear of this, Pilate would surely be punished and removed from office. The priest and Pilate were keenly aware of the vast crowds that were rallying around Jesus. They likely expected a rebellion to follow soon. For these reasons, Jesus was taken in the dark of night, tried in the wee hours of the morning, and taken for crucifixion before most of Jerusalem had much stirred to start the morning."

"Mary," I added, "I heard of Jesus's anger and the chaos he caused in the temple. Everyone was speaking of it on my trip here from Bethlehem. Every traveler wondered if those actions were 'the straw that broke the camel's back,' as you say. It sure seems like it was."

After a long quiet moment of reflection, Mary raised her head, saying, "Aaron, come join us for supper. We'll let you witness a special remembrance Jesus taught us." As we returned to the Upper Room's largest area, all gathered there welcomed me warmly. The room contained far more than Jesus's eleven disciples, his mother, and a few women. Mary said that Jesus's inner circle had now grown to roughly seventy disciples or apostles—many of whom were with me that night in that room. We shared a festive meal of fruits, fish, bread, and wine. After the meal, Peter rose and said that we should take the "Lord's Supper."

Peter recounted that on the night that Jesus was betrayed, he gathered his disciples with him in this very room. After washing their feet and feasting with them, Jesus blessed a loaf of bread, broke it, and handed it to his disciples, saying, "This is my body. As often as you take of this bread, do so in remembrance of me." Peter broke the bread and passed it among us. Each of us took a piece and ate.

After sharing the bread, Peter then took the pitcher, blessed it, and poured its wine into a cup. As he passed the cup, he relayed that Jesus said, "This is my blood, the blood of the covenant that is poured out for many. As often as you take of this cup, do so in remembrance of me." After all of us had taken the Lord's supper, Peter prayed, reminding us of Jesus and his sacrifice for us. After singing a hymn, Mary leaned over and whispered that they had taken the Lord's Supper every night since Jesus's death. I nodded and smiled, thinking what a simple but oh-so meaningful and deeply moving way for us to remember our Christ.

As supper was ending, Mary suggested that I stay in the Upper Room and sleep on the floor on my mat with many of the other men. She said that if I would, tomorrow morning, she would like to take me on her new remembrance ritual. I told her that I looked forward to going with her. I slept soundly, knowing that I was finally beginning to understand, after many decades, what the angels that night had told me.

MARY'S DAILY WALK

Jesus therefore came out, wearing the crown
of thorns and the purple robe. And Pilate
said to them, "Behold the Man."

—John 19:5 (NASB)

E ARLY THE FOLLOWING DAY, after breakfast and prayers, Mary and I left on her new tradition. I asked where we were going. She only smiled, saying, "You will see. We are going on the walk I have made every morning following Jesus's resurrection."

Only a short distance from the Upper Room, we came upon the house of Caiaphas, the high priest. As we walked by, Mary said that upon Jesus's arrest, he was first taken before Annas, the former high priest and the father-in-law of Caiaphas. Annas asked Jesus a few questions but quickly deferred to Caiaphas any actions regarding Jesus.

Jesus was then brought here for his first trial before Caiaphas and his Council of Elders. After much questioning, we understand they asked Jesus if he was the Son of God, and Jesus answered, "You have said it yourself.

Hereafter, you shall see the Son of Man sitting at the right hand of power and coming on clouds of heaven."

"Aaron, those words were the words that the priests and council wanted to hear. To them, Jesus was blasphemous and, in their view, worthy of death. I understand that Caiaphas kept making the case that it was better for one man to die so that the whole of the Jewish faith could be spared and protected. While the priests and councils debated what to do next with Jesus, I understand they kept Jesus here in this home's basement in a cell called 'the Pit.' It gets its name because it is an awful, dark, damp, and small space. It is so tiny and isolated that the prisoner must be lowered into it by ropes. So, Aaron, my Son spent his last human night here in a hole all by himself. What an awful place!"

As we headed north through the town, we came to the palace of Herod Antipas. Mary stated that Antipas, or Herod as he was most often called, lived in Galilee most of the year but came to Jerusalem during major festivals, like Passover. She asked if I had ever heard of a man named John the Baptizer. I said, "Yes, remember, Mary, when I visited you in Bethlehem, you told me of your visit to see your aunt, Elizabeth. You rushed to see her once you learned you were expecting Jesus. I remember so well that an angel announced to Zacharias, John's priestly father, that he and his wife, Elizabeth, were to have a son whose name was to be John. Zacharias laughed and mocked the angel, saying that he and his wife were too old to have children. That doubt caused the angel to strike Zacharias dumb. He did not say another word until John was born nine months later. Soon after John's birth, Zacharias's tongue was loosened. He shouted his joy all over town, saying he would never doubt God again! That is one of my favorite stories. I have told it time and time again to my children and now my grandchildren. Hopefully, they have learned from Zacharias's example: never doubt God!"

Mary nodded, saying, "Yes, yes, I remember. You have a good memory. Well, this house on your right is where Herod Antipas stayed the night of Jesus's arrest. Caiaphas sent Jesus to Pilate's home, which we will pass in a few minutes. Knowing Jesus was a Galilean, Pilate sent Jesus here to be tried by Antipas since both Antipas and Jesus were from the same region. The reason I asked if you knew of John the Baptizer was that Antipas, a wicked, wicked man, was the one who beheaded John. He even served John's head on a silver platter purely to appease his stepdaughter's request. Now he is here judging Jesus. I understand that Antipas pressed Jesus to perform a miracle, but Jesus refused. Antipas continued to mock Jesus by dressing him in a purple robe and a crown of thorns symbolizing royalty. Then Herod, the chief priests, and scribes ridiculed Jesus, calling him King—King of the Jews. I guess when they were tired of their fun, Herod sent Jesus back to Pilate.

"We are approaching Pilate's Antonia Fortress or the Praetorium, as some call it. The word is that Pilate told the religious authorities he could not find any guilt in Jesus, definitely no actions worthy of death. He, instead, offered to punish Jesus and then release him. The priests and their select, handpicked crowd became belligerent, yelling, 'No, Jesus must be crucified.'

"Knowing he was in a dilemma, Pilate turned to a practice that he has used in the past during festivals. Pilate brought Barabbas and Jesus onto that porch you see up there. Have you heard of Barabbas? Barabbas was a man whose hatred and criminal acts caused great fear and loathing, not only among the Romans but also among the Judean citizens. All despised Barabbas. Pilate, standing on that porch, looked down at the crowd, waved to the two prisoners, and offered to set one of them free as a Passover holiday gift. Pilate surely thought the crowd would choose Jesus to be freed versus the hated Barabbas, but he was wrong. Pilate pleaded with the crowd, but they insisted on freeing Barabbas and crucifying Jesus. Unable to sway the crowd, Pilate honored their wishes. He then symbolically and literally washed his hands of the matter and pronounced his decision. Barabbas was set free, and Jesus was sent to his death."

"Mary," I said, "my brother, Dismas, was captured with Barabbas during a robbery. For most of last week, Dismas, Barabbas, and Gestas were held in the same jail near the foot of the Skull. On the morning of the crucifixions, the guards took Barabbas to see Pilate. I thought Pilate would make an example of him and show that no one, not even Barabbas, could harass Rome and get away with it. Shortly after that, Dismas and Gestas were brought to the top of the hill and crucified on the two outer crosses. I was sure that the middle cross was being reserved for Barabbas. Before long, I saw another prisoner amid a procession heading up toward Golgotha. I was certain that man was Barabbas. The courts had declared that Barabbas should die that Friday along with his fellow criminals—my brother and Gestas. After the man in the middle was hanging on his cross, I could finally get close enough to see. I was so shocked to realize that the man was not Barabbas. I did not recognize the man hanging there or put the pieces together until I turned and saw your face. Then I knew the man dying next to my brother was your Son—Jesus. Now I understand why Barabbas was not in the middle. Who would have ever imagined Pilate releasing the hated criminal Barabbas? What irony!"

Mary, shaking her head, turned to the west and continued walking. As we strolled along slowly, she told of how bloodied and weak Jesus was from the beatings. She added, "Jesus's condition, coupled with the weight of the heavy crossbeam he was forced to carry, made it extremely difficult for him to advance toward Golgotha. Each step was extremely difficult. Finally, one of the Roman guards pulled a man from the crowd and forced him to carry Jesus's cross. The man tried to resist, but after looking into Jesus's eyes, he bent down and lifted the beam from Jesus, and carried it to the top of the hill. Thank goodness for that man's kindness and strength. I do not think Jesus would have made it to the top any other way."

As we strolled to the base of Golgotha, "the Skull," I turned to Mary, saying, "Mary, why are you doing this? All of this pain and these disturbing memories. You don't need to put yourself through this. Especially every day. This is too sad."

Mary stopped, asking me to look at her. "Aaron," she said, "You are right that this part is difficult to relive. And it would be were it not for the ending. We need to remember the whole story. As we walk, you will see our frowns will turn to smiles. We still have a way to go to see that all of this evil did not win. Jesus's resurrection tells his followers that there is life everlasting. We need to focus on the paradise that he promised Dismas. Evil does not win. Evil has not won. God's Son, my Son, Jesus, did. As I walk, I am reminded that this journey was part of God's grand plan. There are still many things I do not understand, and I still have much to learn. But I know Jesus tried to teach us how to live and love each other. Most importantly, we are to love God. With his death and with what he told Dismas, I now understand that death is not final. This is why I walk this walk every day that I am in Jerusalem. Wait for the joy which is coming. Are you ready to continue?"

Along the way, Mary continued her story of Jesus's journey to Golgotha. She told of Jesus telling the women surrounding him to weep not for him but weep for themselves and their children, for difficult times were coming for them and the Jewish people. Upon relaying these words, I noticed Mary's frown was still with her. She told of the mocking that Jesus received along the way. He was spit upon, hit by sticks and stones, and mocked as he struggled forward. She said, "How can people be so heartless?"

"Mary," I said, trying to comfort her, "remember this was very early in the morning. Surely, this crowd was hand-picked by the authorities. These were not the people who had been following Jesus. Surely, these were not the people who welcomed him with palm branches and shouts of Hosannah earlier in the week. Most of those followers were just getting up for the day. These were not the people like those in the crowd with me when Jesus preached and then fed the thousands with the meal of one small boy. Those people loved and cared about Jesus. The world is filled with some bad people. I believe that it is filled with far more good people." Mary thanked me, adding, "Some were crying along the way."

As we approached Golgotha, Mary stopped. She could not look to the top. We were to go no further on Jesus's walk as a condemned man that day. After a moment of silent prayer, Mary turned to me with a smile, saying, "Let us go to where love won." She led me down the path on which they carried Jesus's body for burial. As we turned, I glanced up to the top of the hill. To my horror, I saw three other poor souls meeting the same fate as Jesus, Dismas, and Gestas.

The short walk to the tomb was made in silence. Near Golgotha was the tomb of a secret follower, Joseph of Arimathea. Joseph was on the religious council and witnessed the rushed meeting in which the religious authorities judged Jesus and turned him over to Pilate. Mary continued, "Joseph and his friend, Nicodemus, did not vote to condemn Jesus. Instead, Joseph petitioned Pilate to give him the body of Jesus so that he could bury him in his new tomb. Pilate agreed. Joseph and Nicodemus then came to Golgotha, showing the signed petition to the guards.

"After taking my dead Son down from the cross, the guards released his body. These two wonderful men then wrapped his body and then started carrying him away on their mule. That is when you approached me saying you would come to find me. I followed the procession here. When we arrived, the tomb was open with the large sealing stone rolled back. Joseph and Nicodemus then had the body anointed with spices, wrapped in new linens, and placed in this new never-used grave. Aaron, Joseph freely gave his tomb because he believed in Jesus! After a moment of silence and prayer, Joseph said that we could not linger. We had to hurry—sundown was near, and Passover was about to begin."

I told Mary that I had seen Joseph and Nicodemus in their priestly clothes mourning at the base of Jesus's cross. I recalled Joseph then talking to the guard, followed by their attendants taking Jesus's body away. Their example led me to ask if I could take Dismas's body—though I had to bribe the centurion. She stood amazed as I told of rushing to Bethlehem late that afternoon and being able to bury Dismas in our family tomb during the first hour of Passover. We agreed that each of our evening's Passover meals was the saddest, most grief-filled meal we had ever eaten—though neither of our appetites was very strong. She marveled at how much we were able to do in just a few hours but was so pleased to hear that Dismas had received a proper burial.

As we sat in the garden surrounded by many family tombs, Mary relayed that she could not sleep either Friday or Saturday night. She could not clear her mind of Friday's horrors. Early Sunday morning, she awoke as three of Jesus's closest women followers were preparing to leave the Upper Room. They were going to anoint Jesus's body with more herbs and spices. On that awful previous Friday, Joseph and Nicodemus had rushed to get Jesus buried before sundown. While they did what they could, there just were not sufficient hours left to properly prepare the body for burial. The women would now properly anoint Jesus.

The women asked Mary if she wanted to go with them, but Mary refused, saying that she was not ready to handle that sadness. As they prepared to leave, the women questioned how they would roll the heavy stone away so they could enter the tomb. They prayed that a gardener or two would be tending the grounds and would move the rock for them. Mary said the women were committed to doing whatever they could for Jesus—they loved him so.

A few hours later, the women returned to the Upper Room so excited that, at first, they could hardly catch their breath. They had run all the way back. After settling down, they told the disciples, Mary, and the others what had happened. When they got to the tomb's garden, they found it guarded by soldiers, but all of them were paralyzed and motionless. Whether asleep, drunk, or in some form of stupor, they could not tell. Regardless, the women were not stopped as they approached Jesus's grave. As they drew close, they found that the stone had already been rolled away. Why was the tomb opened? Had the soldiers done something to Jesus's body?

With great hesitation and apprehension, they slowly looked through the opening. Inside, the women found a young man sitting on the bench dressed all in dazzling white. The man, surely an angel, told them to not be afraid. He knew they were there to see the crucified Jesus, but Jesus was not there, for he had risen. He was alive, just as he had told them he would be. The women looked at where Jesus had been placed, seeing only his burial shroud, his linens, and the sprinklings of herbs and spices left by Joseph and Nicodemus.

Mary exclaimed, "The angel told them to rush and share this wonderful news with us. On their way back, Jesus greeted them. They hugged him touching his hands and feet. Jesus repeated for them to hurry and tell us. He announced he would visit us later, even in Galilee. Aaron, from this tomb, all men and women throughout the earth can learn that if they only believe in Jesus, they no longer need to fear death. Their spirit will live forever. Each of us can live in paradise with him, just as he promised Dismas. He taught us how to live while on earth. He encouraged us to believe in God and to believe in him as God's Son. With his resurrection, he showed us that we can have life everlasting if we only believe. He showed us how to love. He gave us hope. He is our example of how to live. We should follow him. This spot, right here, is where the race was won—where our frowns turn to smiles. Is this not wonderful? And you and I have witnessed it all—his ministry, his mission from the very beginning! My heart bursts with joy! Aaron, I am so glad you are here. I am so happy you get to see the good news for all people who the angels told you had come."

"Mary, do you remember my telling you that I thought you would be the perfect mother to Jesus when you had those doubts shortly after he was born? And do you remember what the old man told you in the temple when you went there to dedicate Jesus? He said to you that you would be pierced. He was right. Jesus's arrest, crucifixion, and death pierced your heart and soul so deeply. I saw your hurt and your anguish on Golgotha. That man—Simeon was his name, I think—was right! Yes, you have been pierced, but he was also right in that he lived to see the Lord's Christ and God's salvation. Though you were pierced, your joy and excitement today tell me that Jesus has healed your piercing, and you are now whole again.

"When I return to Bethlehem, I promise to study the words of the prophets that told of your Son's coming. I cannot wait to see how Jesus fulfilled those ancient prophecies. I guess our challenge now is to tell others who have not seen and heard what we have so that they can learn about Jesus and make their own decisions. His words at the Lord's Supper are our challenge—everything we do from now on, we should do in remembrance of him. Mary, I promise. That is how I will now live my life—in constant remembrance of him!"

After a long moment of silence and reflection, we headed back to the Upper Room. As we walked, I told Mary that many of my questions had been answered, but I still had so many more. One key question I asked of her remained, "Are you going to be all right? Will you be cared for?"

Mary said, "Do not worry. Remember, while Jesus was on the cross, he told the man with us to take me as his mother, and I was to take him as my son. That man's name is John. He is one of Jesus's most beloved disciples. He will take good care of me. I do not know where we will stay. Maybe here in Jerusalem. Maybe Capernaum in Galilee.

The Lord will instruct us where and when to go. I will be loved and well cared for by John. Do not worry. I will be fine." We agreed that we could discuss the other questions later. Today has been a good day.

When we got back to the Upper Room, Mary joined in preparing the meals to come. I started thinking about my family and my customers. I, too, wanted to share all that I had learned about Jesus. Maybe as I shared the news of Jesus in Bethlehem, word would start spreading. Indeed, it would begin to spread from Jerusalem. During supper, I thanked all of my new brothers and sisters in Christ for their warm welcome and new friendships. I told them of my need to leave for home in the morning. I shared with them how I came to know and love Mary. Their excitement in hearing about that starry night, the angels' message, my visit to the stable, and my repeated visits to see the Holy Family were contagious. They thanked me repeatedly for sharing how their Savior's life on earth had begun. I felt like I had been adopted by a brand-new family.

A Special Invitation and Commission

And Jesus came up and spoke to them, saying, "All
authority has been given to Me in heaven and on
earth. Go therefore and make disciples of all the
nations, baptizing them in the name of the Father
and the Son and the Holy Spirit, teaching them
to observe all that I commanded you and lo, I am
with you always, even to the end of the age."
—Matthew 26:18-20 (NASB)

THE FOLLOWING MORNING, I left for home as Mary
started on her daily Jesus walk. I pleaded that she
send for me if there was anything I could do for her
in the days ahead. She promised she would. With a tender,
long hug, we parted. I found myself hoping and praying
that this was not the last time I would ever get to see her.

Being with Mary gave me a peace that is hard to describe.
I knew why God chose her. She made everyone feel special
and so loved. I ambled slowly back to Bethlehem, finding
that I enjoyed the silence and the time I had to reflect on
all I had witnessed. Although my heart was heavy over the

loss of Dismas, the joy of Jesus's resurrection and knowing that Dismas was with him brought me great joy!

When I got home, I could not wait to share Jesus's story. Hannah, my children, their spouses, and their children all became believers. Some in the village believed; some did not. That was their choice. I felt my new responsibility was to spread the word in hopes that those that heard would accept the promise of paradise.

A few weeks went by, and I got back into my work and daily life routines. I visited the synagogues as often as I could, asking to hear the ancient prophecies of the Messiah. There were many things I did not know about Jesus's earthly life, but all of the prophecies that dealt with the Jesus I knew had come true! Words from hundreds to thousands of years earlier foretelling of the Savior's coming had come to pass, and I had been there to attest its truth. Every day, I was amazed at how all of this came together so perfectly.

Sharing these findings and my experiences led many to believe and accept Jesus as their Savior. The days became even more exciting with news from travelers passing through as they told stories of others who had seen Jesus alive. Their stories shared that he had visited his disciples on a mountain in Galilee and another time while fishing on the Sea of Tiberias. Shared were stories of personal appearances before his half brother James and his lead disciple, Peter. They then said that Jesus had appeared before a crowd of roughly five hundred people. This period was a wonderful, enlightened time for me. They were days of genuine amazement.

After I had been at home for about a month, a young man knocked on our door on a Tuesday looking for me. He said he had a message from Mary. He began by saying, "Do not worry. She is fine. She wants me to share an invitation with you. Jesus has invited his apostles to be with him on the Mount of Olives in two days. Mary would like you to be with them this coming Thursday." I excitedly said yes. The messenger gave me instructions on how to join the disciples and the growing number of apostles. I was to meet them in the Upper Room this coming Thursday morning. I was invited to spend Wednesday with them. I told the young man to tell Mary I would be there. As he left, I prepared my belongings so that I could leave early the following day. I am not sure I slept at all that night. I would see Mary again, but this time, I might get to meet Jesus, my resurrected Lord.

When I joined the followers in the Upper Room around midday on Wednesday, the room was alive with energy. As I went around the room, each person wanted to share his or her story of being in the presence of the risen Lord. Each then seemed to wonder what Jesus wanted them to see or hear. Would Jesus tomorrow, while on the Mount of Olives, call on each of us to do something special? Speculation and excitement filled the dinner conversations, but some anxiety surfaced. Each of us seemed to raise possibilities as to what tomorrow would bring and what our roles would be. After dinner, Peter rose and led in our taking the Lord's Supper. We then turned in for the night. Tomorrow was to be exciting. I wondered if any of us would be able to sleep.

Around the fourth hour the next morning, we gathered, gave thanks for the blessings of the day, and asked that each of us be open and ready for Jesus's message. I know I prayed that I will be deserving of being in Jesus's presence. As we left, I found the silence eerie as each of us was deep in our own thoughts and anticipation. Finally, after a little more than an hour's journey, we reached the Mount of Olives, east of Jerusalem. There were roughly sixty or seventy of us. Peter asked us to be seated and wait. The area we found was green, with grass interspersed among old, twisted, and gnarled olive trees. The day was clear and warm. A gentle breeze blew. The birds chirped, donkeys brayed, lambs and goats bleated. We heard children laughing as they ran on a nearby hill—a peaceful, perfect morning.

As we sat and waited, no one talked. All were excited for Jesus to arrive. We were patient. No one questioned how long we were to wait or if we should have prepared a meal or performed other routine duties to help make the day go smoothly. No, we remained quiet and reflective as we waited on a beautiful day on a beautiful hill outside the Holy City. I believe we all prayed we would be worthy of this day.

After a while—I have no idea how long we waited—Jesus appeared in our midst, holding his hands out from his sides. His nail holes were so starkly visible. Jesus smiled and welcomed us as his brothers and sisters. He prayed, thanking God for each of us and our fellowship with him. He thanked God for our belief and trust in him and our faithfulness. He then told us about the kingdom of heaven. He said, "Do not let your hearts be troubled. You believe in God. Believe also in me. My Father's house has many rooms. If that were not so, would I have told you that I am going there to prepare a place for you? And if I go and prepare a place for you, I will come back and take you to be with me so that you also may be where I am." I remember bursting with joy that I, too, one day would be in paradise with him and Dismas staying in a place he had prepared for me! I thought, "No longer do I have to worry about death. Jesus has conquered that dread." Jesus then reminded us that it was not for us to know the date or time when he would return.

He then turned slowly, looking into each of our eyes. When he looked at me, I felt a warmth and depth and understanding like I have never felt before or since. We were connected. I felt like we were as one. In all of my life, I have never felt such love and acceptance. I know that I cannot do justice in describing how I felt when he looked at me. He looked into my very soul, my very being.

After he had turned and gazed into the eyes of each of us, he raised his hands, and we all stood, so very silently. He said that the Holy Spirit would come upon us. He commissioned us to be his witnesses in Jerusalem, Judea, Samaria, and even in the most remote parts of the earth. He finished, saying, "All authority has been given to me in heaven and on earth. Go, therefore, and make disciples of all the nations, baptizing them in the name of the Father and the Son and the Holy Spirit, teaching them to observe all that I commanded you, and, lo, I am with you always, even to the end of the age." With that, he bowed his head in prayer, raised his arms shoulder high, and was lifted into the air until a cloud hid him. Each of us just stood there in stunned silence and reverence.

In a moment, the cloud dispersed, showing that Jesus had vanished. The clearness and the crispness of the air returned, just as it was before Jesus appeared. As we stood there staring into the sky, two men, dressed all in white, came among us, saying, "Why do you stand looking into the sky? This Jesus, who has been taken up from you into heaven, will come in just the same way as you have watched him go into heaven." And then they, too, were gone.

For the longest while, we stood there still as stones, just looking into the sky. All were in awe and wonder. Other than wind rustling the trees and the birds chirping, not a sound was made. Spellbound is the best way to describe us. I was so wrapped up at the moment that I was totally unaware of my surroundings. I had experienced a moment that would live with me forever.

As I stood there captivated, I remembered the angel's words that Jesus would return just as he had left. I did not want to move, thinking that as sure as I turned or left, Jesus would return. I guess that the others were just like me—caught up in the moment, unsure of what to do, definitely not wanting to miss anything or be the first to change the moment.

Sometime later, I do not know if it was after minutes or hours; I noticed that one and then another of us started putting our arms around the other. We soon formed a large circle. My arms were on Mary, and an older disciple, who I later learned was Bartholomew. As we stood there looking around at each other, I saw tears of joy in the eyes of everyone. I heard whispers of prayers and thanksgiving, but mostly I just heard quietness as each of us tried to take it all in—all of our experiences with Jesus, his life, death, and resurrection. I imagine all were trying to understand what it all meant. I believe most were also doing what I was doing, which was to ask another question, "What am I to do now? How am I to help carry out that commission Jesus just gave us? Am I to spread his word into Samaria?"

After another long while, Peter quietly said, "Praise God." We all joined in, saying, "Praise God." Then Peter started with the Lord's Prayer that Jesus had taught them. I knew most of the words. With heads down, we prayed, "Our Father who art in heaven, hallowed be thy name. Thy kingdom come. Thy will be done on earth as it is in heaven. Give us today our daily bread, and forgive us our debts as we forgive our debtors. And lead us not into temptation, but deliver us from evil. For thine is the kingdom and the power and the glory forever. Amen."

After taking Peter's lead, we each said our prayer of thanksgiving. Then ever so slowly, we started the journey back to the Upper Room. The night included supper, but mostly the night was filled with quiet reverence. None of the chatter or gaiety of an ordinary evening filled that night. Each was in his or her own quiet reverence, basking in the wonder that was Jesus.

The next morning, I thanked the apostles and followers for including me the day before. Before leaving, I asked Mary if we could go outside to sit under a nearby tree. When settled, I said, "Mary, I have been thinking about how the birth of your Son has woven our lives together.

You were with him from birth to his growing into manhood. You witnessed his ministry, his death, and his resurrection. Yesterday, you saw him ascend into heaven. I, too, was there at his birth, death, resurrection, and ascension. I even got to meet him as a boy and hear him preach. We have a bond like no other. Others may have been present for parts, but only you and I can say that we were there from the beginning of his earthly life to its end. We know that yesterday was the end of his earthly stay. Now he lives with his heavenly Father, but for the time he was on earth, only you and I were there from the beginning until yesterday.

"Mary, I am so blessed that God brought me on this journey. I am so blessed to have met you. I feel so unworthy to have been a part of Jesus's earthly stay but so blessed that God included me. I will never forget you. You have shown me so much gentleness, love, and understanding. You, who had doubts when the angel announced God had chosen you to bear his Son, said yes—you were willing to be God's servant. That was so brave. I am amazed at your faithfulness. God chose well when he picked you to be Jesus's mother. My life is so fulfilled by my having met you. My spirit soars that I have seen and now follow my Christ, my Savior. I will pray for you daily and stand ready if you ever need me. God bless you." With that, I hugged Mary, saying I would never forget her.

My life had become defined by her and her Son. One starry night changed my life forever. I was now a member of his new family—one soon to be called Christians. I felt so blessed in so many ways. I hugged her again and said goodbye. As I left and was ready to turn the corner,

I looked back. Mary was still sitting there in the shade of the tree, waving, looking at me with those incredible, loving eyes. My own eyes filled with tears of joy as I headed home. It dawned on me that even a shepherd, one such as I, had a story to tell—even unto Bethlehem and Judea. My story was a most remarkable one—a story that can change lives—the story of my Messiah!

About the Author

AS A LONG-TERM CHRISTIAN and retired executive with Emory University and Emory Healthcare, the author has been wondering for decades what life was like for the shepherd boy following his extraordinary wonders during the Nativity. He serves on numerous committees of the First Baptist Church of Decatur. While interested in autograph collecting, visiting national parks, following baseball (Go Braves!), and reading, this first book just begged to be written. COVID helped the book's creation come to life. The goal of *Even a Shepherd* is to bring the scriptures alive as the reader views Jesus's life through a new and exciting lens. The author lives in Atlanta, Georgia, with his wife, Kay, who painted the book's wonderful cover and suggested the title. Nearby live his children's families highlighted by his five grandchildren.

Printed in the USA
CPSIA information can be obtained
at www.ICGtesting.com
LVHW041253040324
773497LV00010B/276

9 798886 853605